Jayson
GOES FOR IT!

JAYSON
GOES FOR IT!

BRAYDEN HARRINGTON
WITH **DAVID RITZ**

HARPER
An Imprint of HarperCollinsPublishers

Library of Congress Control Number: 2023931283
ISBN 978-0-06-309893-0

Typography by Andrea Vandergrift
23 24 25 26 27 LBC 5 4 3 2 1

First Edition

*This book is dedicated to my family
for always believing in me through good and bad times.*
—B.H.

*To Miss Raisin, my seventh-grade teacher who said,
"Stuttering is nothing to be ashamed of."*
—D.R.

CHAPTER 1

I Know My Name

If there is one word I can say without stuttering, it's the word "here."

"Here" is the first word I've had to say in front of a full classroom on every first day of school since I was seven. In first grade, I could barely get it out. It took a good thirty seconds in third grade, but by fifth grade, it was easy. I can say "here" with perfect fluency. It's the one word I have been able to count on to get me past my speaking jitters, especially now that I'm in eighth grade at Bloom Middle School.

But not this year. Nope. Ms. Wolfson had to be different and change things up on me. We are all supposed to say our names and something about ourselves to the whole home-room class. At least I don't have to go first.

"I'm Chad Callahan. I like to play baseball and go fishing, which I did a lot of this summer."

"Good to meet you, Chad. Next?" Ms. Wolfson says.

I practice my introduction in my head. The annoying thing is, I almost always stutter on my name, "Jayson Linden." I plan to say, "My name is Jayson Linden," since I figure I'll have a better chance of not stuttering on the word "my." Sometimes if I can get a flow going, I can avoid stuttering. That's something my speech therapist taught me.

My friend Preeda is up next.

"I'm Preeda Chantara. I play field hockey and do crafts with my grandmother."

"I'm Seth Greenberg. I like baseball cards."

Thanks a lot, Seth. You can't like them that much or you would have more to say about them. Why are everyone's introductions so short? Can't someone tell a story about something interesting they did over the summer? Why doesn't everyone have a lot more hobbies?

Oh, good. Samantha's next. She's chatty and talks a lot. She'll kill some time.

"Hi! My name is Samantha Hodgkins, and I—"

Samantha suddenly starts coughing loudly, choking on

her own spit or something. She holds her hand up, and Ms. Wolfson gives her a hall pass to go to the nurse. Great. The introductions only seem to go faster from here, and before I know it, Ms. Wolfson's looking at me.

My name is Jayson Linden.

Oops. That was in my head. She's still looking at me.

"Jayson, would you like to introduce yourself?"

I stand up. Maybe I should fake a coughing fit so I can be excused like Samantha. My heart is beating fast. I really don't want to stutter. I would love to start out the year fooling everyone—by being anyone other than the kid who stutters.

"M-m-m . . ."

I get stuck on the "my." My trick doesn't work, which frustrates me even more. I stutter on every word, and I can feel my normally pale face flash red-hot. It takes nearly a half minute for me to say, "M-m-m-m-my n-n-n-n-name is . . ." I can't even get the first consonant sound out.

One of my classmates in the front row laughs and says, "Did you forget your name?"

There's always someone who feels the need to say something mean. This time it's Chad.

Everyone starts cracking up. I'm rattled, but I try to stick it out anyway.

"J-J-Jay . . ." and just when I think I'm going to make it

through my name, Ms. Wolfson interrupts me.

"It's okay, Jayson—"

It's my biggest pet peeve. You think *you* hate getting interrupted? Try on a stutter for a few days and see if you don't hate it ten times more. To my surprise, a voice pipes up behind me.

"L-l-l-let him f-f-f-finish." I turn around to look at the kid who spoke up. A girl I've never seen before is giving me a warm smile. She must be a new student. Is she making fun of me? No, I don't think so.

I can tell when someone is mocking me. People aren't very good about faking a stutter because they don't know how it feels. Even though I've never met another stutterer, she seems to be the real deal.

Ms. Wolfson nods and purses her lips as if to restrain herself from interrupting again. She nods at me to keep going, and I finally get my full name out, but I don't bother with anything else.

When I sit down, the new girls stands up. She doesn't look the least bit worried about taking her turn. In fact, she seems cooler than a lot of the non-stutterers in my class.

"M-m-m-my name is G-G-Gloria L-L-L-Lopez. M-my family m-m-moved here at the b-b-b-beginning of the s-s-summer. I l-l-like d-d-debate, and I-I-I'm n-n-not afraid

4

of c-c-c-controversy. Actually, I like controversy. Actually, I love it. The more controversial, the h-h-h-happier I am."

People laugh, but not because she stutters. Because she's funny. When she's finished, she tosses her dark, shiny hair over her shoulder with a smirk and sits back down. She catches me looking at her and gives me a wink.

The next kid speaks. "I'm Gino Rubato. I like to play soccer."

There are a few students left to give their introductions, but I barely hear them. Who is this new girl, Gloria Lopez? I want to get to know her better.

CHAPTER 2

Hoop

I can't stop thinking about Gloria the rest of the school day. I wanted to introduce myself to her one-on-one after homeroom, but she left the classroom pretty quickly once the bell rang. I kept hoping to see her face in one of my other classes, but unfortunately, we don't have any other classes together. Maybe tomorrow I'll get to homeroom early so I can talk to her.

The last bell rings, and I head to the locker room to change into my clothes for basketball practice. It's about to be the best part of the day because (1) I don't have to talk much, just play, and (2) I get to hang with my best friend,

Chuck. Chuck has a great sense of humor, and we've always gotten along. We've played basketball together ever since we were little kids, and we've been on the same teams together almost as long. He's one of not that many Black kids in our school.

Once I've changed into my basketball clothes, I run into the gym, where I see Chuck practicing his jump shot. "Hey, Chuck," I say, grabbing my own basketball from the ball rack.

"Hey, Jayson. How was your first day?"

"P-p-pretty good."

Just then, I notice Mack Gaines walking into the gym. Mack's the best athlete at school. Mack's about my height— although he was eager to point out that he's got a half inch on me before school let out for summer. He gloats about everything and has been competitive with me ever since he moved here in sixth grade, when I beat him out for the highest GPA in the class. He's super popular, has good grades, and is always a starter as a power forward. Everyone seems to like him, plus his dad is our town's mayor. I even once saw my favorite basketball player, Steph Curry, high-five Mack on ESPN when he was sitting courtside at the Warriors-Celtics game, and I was so jealous.

Mack runs up to us. "Can you dunk?" he asks me right before he does.

"I've been t-t-t—"

"Trying?'" Mack fills in for me, bouncing the basketball up and down.

"Let him finish his own sentence," Chuck snaps, moving to slap the ball away from Mack.

"I don't have time to wait." Mack shrugs, dodging Chuck. He dribbles, hits a layup, and runs over to talk to Coach Croft.

Mack gets on my nerves, but he and Chuck *really* don't get along. Chuck thinks Mack is stuck-up, and he's not afraid to tell him so. I wish I was better at telling Mack when he's being rude.

Coach Croft blows his whistle and starts running us through passing drills before dividing us into teams to practice running plays.

"Jeez, Gaines! Is anyone going to shoot but you?" Chuck shouts as Mack sinks a three-pointer, instead of passing to Chuck or me when we're both wide open.

"The person who's most likely to score is the one who should be shooting." Mack smirks.

"C-c-c-c-cute. I s-s-s-suppose the rest of us should just qu-qu-qu-quit. So you can be the team on your own," I snap.

"Lighten up, Jayson. It's just practice."

I don't say anything else because I am angry, and when

I get mad, my fluency goes out the window. He's right, the stakes aren't high—we're just getting ready for tryouts. But then Mack decides to go straight to the basket instead of passing to me or Chuck—again.

"This is ridiculous!" says Chuck, throwing his hands up in the air.

"Hey, Chuck! It's no big deal," Mack says, holding his palms out in a gesture of surrender. That's a signature Mack move: He makes the other person look like a hothead by shrugging off his own jerkiness like it's just a joke. I can't stand that.

"Gentlemen! Enough!" says Coach Croft, finally stepping in. "Let's all get along, please. Remember, you're on the same team."

For some reason Croft calls us "gentlemen," as if we're all wearing fancy tuxedos instead of a bunch of dudes making fart noises with their armpits. Chuck takes a deep breath, but that isn't the end of it. During the next drill, Mack knocks Chuck over with his shoulder on the way to the basket. And that's that. Chuck springs up from the floor and runs toward Mack, who's sneering smugly. Suddenly Coach is between them. Honestly, I didn't know he could still move that fast.

"Neville, go home and cool off," he says.

"Yeah, all right. I guess it's me," says Chuck, and he walks off the court.

"C-C-C-Coach! That's n-n-not . . ."

"I don't want to hear it's not fair, Jayson. You want to be next?"

Now, if there's one thing I can't stand, it's when people assume they know what I'm going to say. Usually they're not even right. This one time, though, Coach had understood me just fine. It wasn't fair.

CHAPTER 3

Regrouping at Rock 'N Bowl

C huck's home is on top of Rock 'N Bowl—the bowling alley in the same strip mall as our town's Rite Aid and Ace Hardware. It's right next to the barbershop where Dad and I get our haircuts. Even if Chuck weren't my best friend, I would probably still hang out with him for Rock 'N Bowl. It's our second-favorite place in town after the basketball court. The best part is the collection of vintage pinball machines. We're allowed to play them—for free—anytime we want since Chuck's dad, Mr. Neville, owns the bowling alley.

Rock 'N Bowl is a good place to relax and blow off steam,

which is exactly what we do after the first day's tense basketball practice. We head over to our favorite machine, *Mars Attack*. Chuck goes first and scores 150,000 points. The scores are ridiculous in pinball. I figure I am done for, but the pinball forces are with me today as I rack up points on my turn—100,000, then 200,000, then 300,000!

"Watch out! I'm about take over the universe!" I yell gleefully, hitting the pinball controllers.

"Jeez. I forget how fluent you get when you're talkin' trash," Chuck says with a laugh.

I lost my final ball at 325,000.

"And that's that! Bye-bye, earthlings. You had a good run."

"Not bad, but you still didn't beat Dad's high score of five hundred thousand."

"S-save it for another day."

"Let's go eat."

I'm supposed to see my speech therapist, Dr. Dan, at four—his office is about a twenty-minute walk from Rock 'N Bowl. But I'm hungry and tired and today has already been challenging enough between first-day-of-school nerves and basketball practice. A burger takes priority. So we go downstairs to see Big Al, who runs the restaurant inside Rock 'N Bowl. He is as good at making burgers as he is at

H-O-R-S-E, which is saying a lot.

"The usual, Jayson?" asks Big Al.

"Yes, please. Thank you!"

There's almost nothing I'd rather have than one of Al's burgers. The cheese oozes out the sides when you take a bite, and the burger is always super juicy. Al also has this special secret sauce that is creamy and tangy with just a little bit of spice. It's perfection. And he always throws in some extra fries. It's early for dinner, and people have started to wander in to bowl. The pop and rumble sounds of the bowling alley are soothing to me.

I've all but forgotten about the cruddy day I've had. But as we're eating, Chuck asks, "So how'd the rest of practice go without me?"

I swallow my bite of burger and wipe the sauce off my face. "Sh-sh-should have j-j-just left with you," I say.

"Why?"

"I j-j-just hate l-l-looking at Mack's smug face."

"Well, you have to do that anyway," he says.

"Yeah," I say. "But it seems w-w-worse when you're not there. And I don't like how C-C-Coach Croft handled it."

"Dude's always been easy on Mack. He's probably scared of what Mack might tell Mayor Gaines."

"Being the m-m-mayor's son sure has its privileges," I say.

"Yeah, but it means you're always the mayor's son. Mack will never know who he is or what he's capable of on his own."

"I g-g-guess that's true." I just wish Mack would leave me and my friend alone.

Soon Chuck and I start talking about our favorite basketball players and challenge Big Al to a game of H-O-R-S-E outside, and I put Mack and my appointment with Dr. Dan out of my mind.

CHAPTER 4

Bummer #1

The next morning, I wake up a little late, so Dad drives me to school.

Dad and I are super close. My mom died right after I was born, so it's always been just me and Dad. I'd love to have a mother. Everyone wants a mother. But maybe because I never knew my mom, I can't say I miss her. Besides, Dad's a cool guy. We almost always get along great.

"Did you forget about your appointment with Daniel yesterday?" he asks in the car. He and Dr. Dan are friends, so I think it's hard for Dad to call him "Dr. Dan."

"Oh . . . uh, yeah. Sorry."

"You forgot about it?" He stops at the light and looks at me.

"I g-g-guess so."

"Really?"

"I had a c-c-crappy d-d-d-day. I j-j-j-just didn't f-f-feel like breathing exercises and l-l-l-lectures about f-f-fluency."

"Well, I hope you feel like it this afternoon because I rescheduled your appointment. You're lucky he had space and could fit you in."

"Yeah. I f-f-f-feel r-r-really lucky."

Dad hates it when I'm sarcastic, but I hate going to Dr. Dan even more.

I get to homeroom just barely on time. The new girl, Gloria, smiles at me as I slide into my seat, and I smile back. I wish I could talk to her, but I don't have a chance. Later on in the day, though, when classes are over, I run into her in the hallway as she's grabbing books from her locker.

Gathering my courage, I walk over to her. "Hi!" I say. "Remember me?"

"That's a s-s-s-silly question," she says.

"Why?"

"Because you know the answer is y-y-yes."

"Where are you g-g-g-going?" I ask as she shuts her

locker and starts walking down the hallway in the opposite direction.

"Debate. Want to come with me?" she asks.

"Only if I d-d-d-d-don't have to talk at debate." I say, walking beside her.

"You d-d-d-d-don't have to t-t-talk," she says.

I'm glad. I'm also curious to see how she handles her stutter in a situation like this. She opens the door to Mr. Talbot's classroom. He's the history teacher and the debate coach. We must be just a little late, because there's a full group already, including Mack. Everyone's still chatting among themselves, but Mack looks surprised to see me.

"Jayson! Are you joining debate?" he asks.

"J-j-j-just checking it out. I'm n-n-not sure yet."

Mr. Talbot comes in, and there are three students still engrossed in conversation. Mack turns to them.

"Hey, guys! Looks like it's time to get started." As usual, he seems to think it's his job to run the show. I try not to roll my eyes.

"Thanks, Mack. This isn't my first rodeo," says Mr. Talbot, "I think I can handle things from here. Welcome, everyone."

Mr. Talbot explains how debate works and then talks about who the team will compete with.

"If we successfully compete against the other schools in

our county, we'll go up against the rest of the state."

Gloria smiles at me as if she's excited, but just the thought of having to talk in front of an auditorium full of people makes my palms sweat. This is probably my first and last debate experience. I'm happy to just be Gloria's cheering section.

"We're going to start with a little warm-up just to show those of you who are new how a debate works and allow the rest of you to get your brains and vocal cords back into the game. Our subject will be 'Should kids be allowed to have use of their cell phones during school hours?' I'll allow you five minutes to prepare. We'll flip a coin to pick pro and con."

Mack, Gloria, and David Wentworth are arguing for the con side. Mr. Talbot tries to put me on their side, but I explain I'm just watching for now and he seems okay with that.

The pro group makes an argument that concerns students' rights and how we rely on cell phones in case of an emergency. Helen Davies makes an interesting point about how it doesn't matter if a person likes the idea of a cell phone or not. The fact is that they are here, and kids have them. It's more practical to make rules about their usage than it is to ban them.

Mack and Gloria as the opposing group argue that cell

phones are an unnecessary distraction.

Mack is a strong speaker, but Gloria puts together the most compelling argument. The timer goes off, though, in the middle of her talking.

"We have enough d-d-d-distractions during the day without our phones. Social m-m-m-m-media is highly addictive. S-s-s-students receive a d-d-dopamine hit not unlike that in the use of a c-c-c-controlled substance. If cell phones are in-in-inevitable, as H-H-H-Helen s-s-says, then wh-wh-wh-why d-d-don't w-w-we just give up?"

Gloria looks a little thrown by the bell going off in the middle of her argument. But she continues anyway and finishes her point.

Then the groups switch their positions. Group one argues pro; group two argues con. Again, Gloria is great.

"School has the r-r-r-r-right to have us turn off our phones during class," she says, "but n-n-n-n-no business denying us access to them during r-r-r-recess or lunchtime. This infringes on our p-p-p-p-personal rights." From there, she gets more detailed. I'm sure everyone agrees that she's won the argument. She's the best debater in the room.

After the debate is over, Mack raises his hand.

"Mr. Talbot," he says, "we have a strong team this year."

"I agree," says the teacher.

"That's why I think Gloria would be great helping us do research, but maybe she shouldn't be a speaker. The rules only give you five minutes to argue. Gloria took seven minutes arguing pro and eight minutes arguing con. She kept talking after you rang the bell."

"Well," says Mr. Talbot, "it is the first debate of the year. We all need a little latitude."

"But at the tournaments, the judges won't be so generous. And that means points will be deducted. We'll never win."

Mr. Talbot scratches his chin for a moment. Then he says, "Does anyone think Mack has a point?"

A few other students nod.

I shake my head. "N-n-no!" I shout. "Gloria m-m-makes strong arguments. She sh-sh-should be allowed to p-p-p-present them. Sh-sh-she was better than anyone else on the team!"

"Jayson isn't even in this club," says Mack. "He's just here to watch."

I'm annoyed, but what can I say? He's right.

"Would you be disappointed if you helped us research instead of debating?" Mr. Talbot asks Gloria.

"V-v-very much so," Gloria answers.

The teacher picks up the rule book governing debates and looks over it. This takes several minutes. Tension builds.

Finally, he puts down the book and addresses the class.

"I see no exceptions for speech impediments here," he says. "Gloria, I would love to have you work with us as a researcher. But I'm not sure yet if the rules of debate will allow for . . ."

Gloria doesn't wait for him to finish. "A s-s-stutterer?"

"I may have to look into it further."

"W-w-well. Until then. . ." She gets up and storms out of the room. I run after her.

"Hey, Gloria, wait! Maybe we can ask the student c-c-c-council to write the state debate board," I say, trying to comfort her.

"There is no student council yet," she says, her eyes filled with tears. "Elections haven't been h-h-h-held. Elections for president and vice president aren't until November. But by then, it'll be too late."

"Then we can write the b-b-b-board as individual students."

"By the time the board gets around to it, d-d-debate season will be over," she says.

I don't know what to say, so I don't say anything. I just stand there as she turns and runs down the hallway and out the school's front door.

CHAPTER 5

Dr. Dan

I'm still mad about what happened to Gloria when I walk to my session with Dr. Dan. He's the last person I want to see, actually. If I'm having any kind of stress at all, therapy seems to make my stuttering worse, and Dr. Dan is a little intimidating.

He calls me into his office precisely at 4:00 p.m., and as always, he's wearing a bow tie. This one is navy blue.

"First week of school," he says when I sit down. "How'd it go, Jayson?"

"M-m-m-mixed."

"You want to tell me why?"

"My new friend G-G-G-Gloria didn't make the debate team. Not because she's not a g-g-great debater. She is. But only b-b-b-b-b-because she stutters. You only get five minutes to argue, and it t-t-t-t-takes her longer."

"You're a good friend," says Dr. Dan.

"Wh-wh-wh-why?" I ask.

"I can see you're very upset. It shows how much you care."

"I'm upset b-b-b-b-b-b-b-b-because I don't know what to d-d-d-do about it."

"My hope is that it will motivate you to do more to apply the strategies we've been working on here. If Gloria had found the kind of fluency you want, this problem would not have arisen."

"But Gloria d-d-d-d-d-d-deserves to be on the d-d-d-d-d-d-debate team with or without f-f-f-fluency, don't you think?" I snap. Why doesn't Dr. Dan understand?

"I'm not the debate team adviser."

"But if you were, wh-wh-what would you d-d-d-do? T-t-t-take the advice of a s-s-student? B-b-because that's what Mr. T-T-Talbot did."

I couldn't believe what Dr. Dan was saying. Gloria deserved to be on the team!

"I guess he would have to take into consideration the bylaws of debate procedure."

"So you think Gloria sh-sh-sh-sh-sh-sh-should not be on the t-t-t-t-team?"

"I didn't say that, Jayson."

"So what d-d-d-d-d-did you say, Dr. Dan?"

"I'm saying it's best if we concentrate on you—and the progress you've made toward fluency," Dr. Dan says calmly.

"Does that mean that k-k-k-k-kids without f-f-f-f-fluency shouldn't ever be allowed to d-d-d-d-debate?" I ask, trying to keep my voice from rising.

"I feel like you've come here today to debate *me*, Jayson." He smiles as if he's making a little joke, but there's nothing funny about what he's saying.

Dr. Dan doesn't understand how smart Gloria is. And just as I was afraid of, I'm too wound up for speech therapy. But I already bailed on one session, so I don't say anything. I don't want Dr. Dan going back to my dad and telling him that I'm being uncooperative.

For the rest of the session, Dr. Dan has me read out loud certain parts of a book with words I usually stutter on.

"See if you can be aware of your breath as you approach those words," he says. "See if you can gently articulate those words. See if you can see those words as your friends, not your enemies."

"Okay," I say. But when I come to those words, I keep

stuttering. And not only do I stutter, I think how much I hate stuttering. If it wasn't for stuttering, Gloria wouldn't have to go through what she's going through. She would get to be on the debate team. And I wouldn't have to keep seeing Dr. Dan.

I'm frustrated and angry—at my dad who makes me see Dr. Dan, at Mack for hurting my friend Gloria, at Mr. Talbot for going along with Mack. I'm mad at everyone.

CHAPTER 6

Bummer #2

B asketball tryouts are held at the end of my second week at school. Twenty of us show up, but only fifteen will make the team. And tension keeps building between Mack and Chuck.

Coach Croft starts us out with some drills—sprints up and down the court, catching and passing the ball, dribbling past opponents—until it's time for a scrimmage. The best five players—which, of course, includes Mack—against five others. Chuck and I are among the others. For the first five minutes, we hold our own, but then Mack and his boys start to dominate and score basket after basket on us.

Coach Croft blows the whistle and sends me and Chuck to the bench so he can bring in the next set of boys. They do worse than us. Then Coach switches up substitutions. Chuck and I are sent back in, then back out.

When the game is finally over, Mack stands next to the coach on the sidelines, whispering in his ear. Coach nods. What could Mack be telling him?

"Okay, fellas," says Mr. Croft, "I've decided something that's going to make it easier for the Bloom Bobcats to work as a team. I'm reducing the total number of eligible players to twelve."

I raise my hand.

"Jayson, do you have a question?"

"Yes, wh-wh-wh-wh-why are you d-d-d-d-d-doing that?"

"Mack reminded me that the van taking us around to road games can't hold that many guys."

"Can't we get another van?" I ask. "And besides, what about home games? We don't need any v-v-v-v-vans for home games."

"It's going to be easier to have one van of twelve players rather than fifteen. So I'm going to call out the twelve names of those I've chosen for the team."

Mack is called first. I'm called twelfth. Chuck isn't called at all.

I can't believe it, and when I look over at Chuck, his face has fallen. He's too stunned to speak.

I raise my hand again.

"What is it, Jayson?" asks Mr. Croft.

"If Chuck isn't on the team, I don't want to be on the t-t-t-t-team either."

"We need you on defense, Jayson," says Coach.

"Jayson, just let it go," Chuck says sharply. He grabs his bag and walks out of the gym, shaking his head.

"So we'll see you at practice next week?" Croft says to me.

"Why ch-ch-change to twelve players now?" I ask Croft. "It's always been f-f-f-fifteen."

"I've already explained, Jayson. I'm not going to do it again," Croft says. "Will I see you at practice?"

Mack is looking over his shoulder at us as he leaves. He smirks at me, and I glare back at him.

"Yeah, I'll be there."

I grab my stuff and catch up with Chuck, who's standing outside waiting for his mom to pick him up.

"Mack p-p-p-pulled one of his sleazy m-m-maneuvers," I tell Chuck. "He knows the coach l-l-l-loves him and will l-listen to anything he says. I don't want to play on a team without you. And I definitely don't want to be on h-h-his team. Maybe I just won't go."

"You're on the team, Jayson. That's it. You wouldn't let me quit if it were the other way around," he says. Chuck gives me a stubborn look. I can tell nothing I say will change his mind.

I pause for a minute.

"Right?" he presses.

I refuse to say yes. But he's right. I wouldn't.

That's why Chuck is my best friend. He knows how much I want to play, and he won't let anything get in my way. But I don't want to play without my best friend and teammate. We have to find a way to fix this.

CHAPTER 7

The Glass Box

After the disaster of basketball tryouts, I cannot wait to get home. My dad designed our house himself. He calls it "the glass box," which is pretty appropriate. It's compact but has everything we need, and it looks pretty cool. As you might have guessed from the name, it's a cube two stories high with floor-to-ceiling windows on all sides. We live right on the edge of Oaks, a section of the town that's hilly and green. When it's sunny, it's great. And when there are storms, it's even better. I love watching the dark clouds and the rain crashing against the glass. We live inside, but it feels like we're outside. We can be in the middle of a storm without getting wet.

Even when everything else stinks, I can count on home to make me feel a bit better, and home, most of all, means my dog, Caitin. As soon as I walk in the door, I hear her nails scraping against the floor as she races toward me and she wiggles all over with excitement. It's like a full-body smile, and it's super infectious. She runs back into the hall to grab her favorite toy, a squeaky stuffed squirrel, and brings it to me, her floppy brown-and-black ears trailing behind her.

"Hey, girl! I missed you," I say, throwing the squirrel across the kitchen and into the dining room. She bounds over, grabs it, and brings it back.

"Good girl! How was your day, huh?" I crouch down and scratch behind her ears, and she flops over on her back for a belly rub. "Oh yeah, that's the good stuff." I never stutter when I talk to Caitin. She's the best listener.

Dad gets home a few minutes after I do. He's got burgers from Big Al's. I put out some plates and napkins and a pitcher of water, and we sit down to eat. He asks me about tryouts.

"Chuck got c-c-c-cut from the team," I say.

"What? You're kidding?"

"Nope. C-C-C-C-Coach decided t-t-t-twelve players was

enough. F-f-f-fifteen don't f-f-fit in the van."

"Really? That's odd reasoning."

I tell him about Mack whispering to the coach and how Mack and Chuck have been butting heads in practice. Then we talk about debate and Gloria and how Mack got Gloria disqualified for the team.

"It does seem like Mack may be exerting undue influence."

"You think?" I ask.

"Well, look. I don't know if Coach Croft and Mr. Talbot even realize that they're doing it. But Mack can be charming—and it seems like he's also pretty persuasive."

"Exactly."

Dad can sense that I'm annoyed, and he changes the subject to the upcoming Golden State Warriors game. They're playing against the Celtics, and Dad's getting tickets from Dr. Dan. We talk about the Warriors and the last season and their past matchups and make bets about who will win and what the score will be. He says the Warriors will win by two; I say they'll win by at least ten. Dad says if I'm right we can have Big Al's twice next week, and if he's right, I have to help him weed the garden next weekend. The stakes are high. Still, I feel a little bit better, just like I always do after talking to Dad.

CHAPTER 8

Hail to the Chief?

On Saturday night, I invite my friends over for pizza. I look forward to it all day long, even when I'm cleaning my room. It'll be nice to just chill, play video games, and maybe watch TV. I'm tired of the drama of school and Mack Gaines. The fictional drama of a TV show is much more entertaining.

Chuck and his dad pick up Gloria on the way, so they arrive together. Chuck and I have been sitting with Gloria at lunch and we all get along great. Gloria kicks our butts at *Mario Kart* three times before the pizza arrives. Finally, Chuck says, "I vote we switch games."

"Wanna watch *Invincible*?" I ask.

I like a lot of superhero shows, but *Invincible* is my current favorite. I've already seen every episode in the first season, but I'm happy to rewatch them with Gloria and Chuck. Then we get to the part where Todd the bully comes in and starts harassing Amber.

"This reminds me of Mack," says Chuck.

"A little. Mack's a little more s-s-s-subtle, but maybe just as pushy. He's still the most p-p-p-p-popular kid in our class," I say.

My idea in watching *Invincible* was to get our minds off what happened at school. But I've done just the opposite.

The pizza arrives as we're talking.

"You're right, Jayson" says Gloria. "Mack is s-s-s-subtle. He gets everyone to d-d-d-do what he wants in a sn-sn-sneaky way."

"That's what he did with Coach Croft," says Chuck.

"And Mr. Talbot. They don't seem to realize it's happening. They j-j-j-j-just d-d-d-do what he w-w-wants," Gloria says.

Chuck says, "You know, of course, that Mack is already telling everyone he's running for class president. And his girlfriend, Suzy Best, is running for vice president. He thinks

34

he's going to win unchallenged and doesn't think anyone else will run."

"G-g-get ready for P-President Mack," I say.

"And VP S-S-S-Suzy," says Gloria. "Suzy's a ch-ch-ch-ch-cheerleader."

"When is the election?" I ask.

"Just b-b-b-before Thanksgiving," says Gloria.

"I have an idea," says Chuck.

"What?" asks Gloria.

"Jayson should run for president."

"It'll b-b-b-barely be a competition," I say. "Mack will win before it even st-st-st-starts."

"Don't be so sure," says Chuck.

"J-J-J-J-Jayson, you *should* run for president," Gloria says.

"Exactly! Everyone loves you, Jayson. You could totally beat Mack!" says Chuck.

"No!" I blurt out.

"Why not?" asks Gloria.

"Because I'd l-l-l-lose."

"I'm n-n-n-not so sure you would," says Gloria. "A lot of the k-k-k-kids seem to like you."

"Tons more kids l-l-l-l-like Mack," I say.

"Gloria's right. Everyone likes you, Jayson! And if they

don't, well . . . we'll change their minds," says Chuck.

"How are we going to d-d-d-d-do that?" I ask.

"By b-b-b-being smart," says Gloria. "By b-b-b-being smarter than Mack."

"When I l-l-l-l-lose, I'll feel terrible," I say. "And besides, I'd have to m-m-m-make lots of speeches. I don't want to m-m-m-m-make any speeches."

"Can't your speech therapist help you?" asks Chuck.

"He never helps me," I say.

"Then t-t-t-t-try mine," says Gloria.

"What's the d-d-d-d-difference between yours and mine?" I ask.

"I don't know. But it can't hurt for you to m-m-m-m-meet her."

"Well, I'd have to ask my dad," I say. "And I'll think about the whole running-for-president thing."

Gloria and Chuck high-five, and I'm glad when we all turn back to the TV. Could I really run for class president?

Later, after my friends leave, I'm sitting in my bed reading for class, when Caitin jumps up to be next to me.

"That dog is devoted to you, Jayson," Dad says as he leans against the frame of my bedroom door.

"Caitin is a champ. Can I ask you a question?"

"Shoot."

I take a deep breath. "Dad, what do you think of the idea of m-m-m-me running for class president?"

Dad thinks for a moment, then says, "If that's something you want, sure. Go for it."

"I'd be running against M-M-Mack Gaines."

"Whatever you decide, Jayson, I'm behind you."

"Okay," I say, but I'm still not sure. "Also, Dad, Gloria has a speech therapist she r-r-r-really likes. Is it okay with you if I see her?"

"What's wrong with Dan?"

"I'm n-n-n-n-not sure Dr. Dan is helping me all that much."

"And you've told him that?"

"I don't want to hurt his feelings. He's y-y-y-your friend."

"And Gloria's therapist has helped her?"

"I think so."

"Well, I can't see any harm in letting you try out some-one else—as long as the therapist has the right credentials."

"You can call Gloria's m-m-m-mom, Mrs. Lopez, to check."

"Okay, I'll call her tomorrow, and we'll get it figured out. Good night, Jayson. Don't stay up too late reading."

"Night, Dad."

Dad kisses me on the forehead and then leaves. I go back to reading the novel that Mr. Ritchie, my English teacher, assigned, *To Kill a Mockingbird*. I like the character of Atticus, who, like my father, is a single dad. He's a brave lawyer fighting bigotry. He takes on the whole town to stand up for what's right. That gets me to thinking—do I have the bravery to take on the whole school since Mack practically runs it already? I look outside and see that a light drizzle has turned into a deluge. The sky has broken open, and rain is coming down in sheets. The weather excites me. It's unpredictable. I like things that you can't predict. I wonder if that's true of the election for class president. I'm not sure.

With Caitin next to me, I fall asleep quickly but, in the middle of the night, I wake up frightened. In my dream, I am runnning for president. The whole school is in the auditorium waiting to hear me speak. I open my mouth, and I can't talk. I can't get a single word out.

CHAPTER 9

Questions, Questions, Questions

Chuck and I are in the same English class. On Monday before class starts, Chuck slides into his desk next to mine and asks me if I've made up my mind about running for class president.

"Nope."

"But you thought about it?"

"Yep. Even d-d-d-dreamed about it."

"How was the dream?"

"Nightmare."

"Uh-oh."

Just then, our teacher, Mr. Ritchie, arrives and starts the

discussion about *To Kill a Mockingbird*. He doesn't call on me, thankfully. I don't want to talk. I never want to talk, which makes it all the more ridiculous that I'm considering running for president. If I didn't have to speak, it would be easier. I wouldn't have to be the person who stutters. That would be some campaign slogan: "Elect the stutterer: No more smooth talk."

Mr. Ritchie asks us how we feel about what happened to Tom Robinson in the story.

Chuck raises his hand. "The same way I feel when I read the news and another Black man gets blamed for something he didn't do. It's not like I haven't felt it before. It's not like that stuff isn't still going on. People always blame the Black guy. Not much has changed."

Chuck and I have talked about this before, but all of a sudden, I realize something. If I don't want someone to think about me as a stutterer, all I have to do is avoid talking. It's not easy, but it can be done. Chuck can't avoid being Black. He has to be brave just to get out of bed in the morning. And then there are all the times he's stuck up for me. Maybe I can handle making a speech or two after all.

After school, I have a session with Dr. Dan. At least I'll have something new to talk to him about.

At 4:00 p.m. sharp, Dr. Dan calls me into his office. He's wearing one of his signature bow ties. Today it's flaming red. We sit down, facing one another in those matching chairs.

"Good to see you, Jayson. Your dad mentioned something about you wanting to run for class president."

"I'm thinking about it, but I haven't made up my m-m-m-mind."

"I'm not sure it's a good idea."

I'm surprised and a little angry.

"How c-c-c-come?" I ask.

"Well, to be candid, Jayson, I'm not sure you're quite ready for that amount of public speaking. At this point, you might find it frustrating. On the other hand, I have no doubt that a year from now, when you're further along, you'll be fully prepared. Meanwhile, we can use this year to drill down on the techniques that will turn you into a fluent speaker."

"S-s-s-s-so I should just f-f-f-f-f-forget about it?"

"For the moment. A setback at this point would not be helpful."

I stay silent. I'm feeling really uncomfortable.

"The other thing your dad mentioned was Dr. Sylvia Fine."

"Who is sh-sh-sh-she?" I ask.

"The speech therapist you wanted to see."

41

"Oh, right, yes. She's my friend Gloria's therapist."

"I gather so. Dr. Fine has a PhD in psychology. Speech therapy is only one of her specialties, and so her experience is limited. I think exposing you to another kind of treatment at this time would be confusing."

"Well, Dad s-s-s-s-s-said it was okay."

"He said it's your choice."

I'm feeling firm when I say, "If it's my choice, I'll see her—at l-l-l-least once."

"If that's what you want," Dr. Dan says. He smiles, and I can tell he's not happy. But I don't care. I'm curious to meet Dr. Fine.

CHAPTER 10

Meeting Dr. Fine

On Thursday, Gloria invites me to her house after school so we can help each other with our math homework. She lives in a two-bedroom apartment with her parents and her younger sister, Blanca. Both her parents are nurses at a hospital in Oakland, and they're really cool.

When we get to Gloria's, Mrs. Lopez is in the middle of making a huge pot of paella with shrimp and scallops.

"That smells so good, Mrs. Lopez," I say.

"Join us for dinner, Jayson?" Mrs. Lopez asks.

"I'll call and ask my d-d-d-d-d-d-d-d-dad," I say. "But I'm sure it'll be okay."

"Good," says Gloria, "then you can go with me to speech therapy at five. Do you still want to m-m-m-m-meet her?"

"Yes."

We speed through our math homework before watching some funny TikTok videos. By then, it's time for therapy. Mrs. Lopez drives us over to a medium-sized medical building across the street from a huge Home Depot. My dentist has his office there. We walk up to the third floor. The office door says *Counseling Services* and *Dr. Sylvia Fine*. We wait on a couch in the reception room, still messing with TikTok on my phone, when a woman appears. She has a broad face, cheeks with dimples, and streaks of blue in her blond hair. I'm a little surprised by those streaks of blue. She looks pretty young.

"You must be Jayson," she says. "I'm Sylvia. Gloria said you might be coming. I'm so pleased."

We follow her to her office filled with an assortment of plants. On one wall is a poster from a Taylor Swift concert; on another wall, a painting of three men in robes sitting around a campfire. She sees me staring at it.

"Who do you think they are?" she asks.

"I'd g-g-g-guess Jesus, Buddha, and Moses."

"You guessed right! Here's a granola bar!"

She actually reaches into her desk and hands me a granola bar.

"That painting was done by my nephew," she says. "He saw the scene in a dream. So my first question to you, Jayson, is about Moses. Did you know he stuttered?"

"No."

"Well, he did. And, as you might have noticed, he made quite a name for himself in spite of it. Or maybe because of it. I have a feeling he was a man who found peace with his stutter. Have you ever heard of such a thing?"

"Ha! No," I say.

"Few people have. Gloria, you don't mind if I tell your friend Jayson about the conversation we had last week, do you?"

"Not at all. Go ahead," says Gloria.

"Well, Jayson, Gloria called me last week after the incident at her debate class. She was quite upset. She was crying. She was also really angry. At that moment, she didn't like being a person who stutters. Is that right, Gloria?"

"I hated b-b-b-b-being a person who stutters."

"Of course! You love debating. You're good at debating. But because you're a person who stutters, you were told that you couldn't participate in public debates. So it's no wonder that you were angry."

"Absolutely," I say. "S-s-so was I!"

"And so was I!" Sylvia says. "And as people who stutter, you both have every right to be furious. What your adviser did was unacceptable, Gloria. I have no qualms about being angry at him. We all should be angry at him. But being angry at your stutter is a different matter. Your stutter is part of who you are."

"B-b-believe m-me, I n-n-never forget that," I say.

"It's part of who you are, but it doesn't need to be all of it. Right?" Sylvia says. I don't respond. I think about what she is saying—about what it means that the stutter is just part of me.

"Th-th-that's why we don't say 's-s-stutterer.' We say 'person who s-s-s-stutters,'" Gloria continues.

"That way it describes something about you, but it doesn't define you," Syvlia explains. "You and Gloria are much more than people who stutter. You're good students and loyal friends. Gloria likes debate; you play basketball. You just also happen to be people who stutter."

The rest of the session goes by in a blur. Sylvia speaks so quickly, and with so much enthusiasm, I can't help but like her. I think about our conversation all the way back to Gloria's. I feel excited and confused. With Dr. Dan, I focused on my stutter so much that it seemed to be all that mattered. Even when I want to talk about other things with him—the election, basketball—he's always quick to bring the conversation back to "The Stutter." I had never thought about it being something that didn't define me. It seemed like I didn't have a choice.

"D-d-d-do you hate your stutter?" I ask Gloria.

She's quiet for a long time, thinking about it. Finally, she answers.

"It's h-h-h-h-hard for me n-n-n-n-not to hate my stutter," she says. "At least when it k-k-k-k-keeps me from doing what I want to do."

"I kn-kn-kn-know what you mean."

"B-b-b-b-but it's okay, right? You kn-n-n-now it's okay to stutter?"

"What do you m-m-m-mean by okay?" I ask.

"Th-th-there's nothing wrong with stuttering. N-n-n-n-not really. It's inconvenient. And f-f-f-frustrating sometimes. B-b-b-b-but the only r-r-reason we hate it is because n-n-n-not everyone does it. B-b-but why hate what makes you unique."

No one has ever made me think about my stutter this way before. Suddenly I'm on the outside of it, observing. And I'm talking to someone else with a stutter. It's never been easy for me to separate myself from my stutter. When I'm angry about stuttering, I'm angry at myself. But knowing someone who stutters, someone I like and admire, someone who's smart and good at arguing, and who can beat me at video games—it changes everything. It separates the stutter from the person.

"You're r-r-right," I say.

"Y-y-y-you know I t-t-t-talked to Mr. T-T-T-Talbot."

"Yeah?"

"H-h-h-he's agreed to let Mack and me debate about wh-wh-wh-whether p-p-p-people who stutter should be allowed to debate.

"Th-th-th-that's f-f-f-fantastic! Y-y-you're amazing!"

"Y-y-y-you don't think I know that?"

"P-p-p-pardon me! I forgot I was in the presence of g-g-g-greatness."

Gloria laughs and then is quiet for a minute.

"Wh-wh-wh-what I w-w-wanna know is, wh-wh-wh-where do you stand on the election?" she asks.

"Ugggghhh! Y-y-y-you r-r-really don't g-g-give up, do you?"

"Nope. I th-th-think the deadline to d-d-d-declare candidacy is next week."

Maybe it will change when I'm not sitting next to Gloria anymore, but right now I'm feeling pretty invincible. But I still have to think about it. I'm still not sure.

CHAPTER 11

Vote for Jay!

I have a practice the next day, and, inspired by Gloria advocating for herself, I approach Coach Croft afterward to stick up for Chuck.

"What's up, Jayson?"

"I j-j-j-just w-w-want to ask you to reconsider the number of players on the team."

"Reconsider?" he says. "Jayson, I've been your coach for three years, but I've been a coach for much longer. I know you and Chuck are friends and you want him on the team with you. But I don't want any more feuding between players."

"B-b-but Mack . . ." I start to argue, but he holds up his hand and stops me.

"You know it's not the first time. Twelve is a good number. You guys can be a good, tight group and play well together."

I stand there fuming for a minute, then I turn to go. I know anything that comes out of my mouth will be a hash.

"This is the last of it, Jayson."

On Monday, Chuck has to talk to Ms. Barnard, our bio teacher last period, so we meet up afterward and slip into the back row of Gloria's debate a little late. Because he thinks it will be good practice, Mr. Talbot holds the debate in the auditorium rather than his classroom. The stage is the center, and the seating area is raked so the debaters and the moderator—Mr. Talbot—are sitting below us. Mack is to the right of Mr. Talbot, and Gloria is to the left. I never noticed before, but Mr. Talbot has an oversize Adam's apple. As he speaks, it bobs up and down like a yo-yo. His voice, though, is deep and rich. I'm pretty sure he used to be an actor.

"Today I've agreed to supervise a debate that should prove interesting," he says. "For the sake of fairness—and I do believe in fairness—I want to give Gloria Lopez the chance to defend her position to join our other debaters. So, the proposition is simple: As a member of a debate team, should a stutterer be given special consideration? Gloria will take the pro position. And Mack will rebut."

Gloria raises her hand.

"Yes, Gloria?" says Mr. Talbot.

"I object to the fr-fr-framing of the proposition."

"Why?" asks the teacher.

"Because I am not asking for special c-c-c-c-consideration."

"Then what are you asking?"

"Simply," says Gloria, "that, based on my knowledge of the issues, I b-b-be allowed to join the d-d-d-debate squad."

"Well, given the fact that you are a stutterer . . ."

"I p-p-prefer to call myself a person who stutters."

Mack calls out, "Hey, we're debating about the debate, and the debate hasn't even started. This is really going to be good."

The room roars with laughter. I don't laugh, and neither does Chuck.

"Okay, Gloria," Mr. Talbot concedes. "I apologize. I am happy to refer to you as a person who stutters and will modify my proposition as such: As a member of a debate team, should a person who stutters be given special consideration?"

Gloria begins to argue again, but Mr. Talbot stops her.

"Gloria, you now have five minutes to make your case."

Gloria is flustered. I can feel her anger. The debate question is tilted against her. So is most of the audience. She sees, though, that she has no choice. I can't help but admire her for having the guts to take on Mr. Talbot and Mack in front of everyone.

She stands up and faces Mr. Talbot and all the students. As she starts, she stutters very severely, so severely that when the bell rings indicating that her five minutes are up, she's only halfway through her argument.

Mack's turn.

Addressing our class, he speaks through a smile. A confident smile.

"Thank you, Mr. Talbot, for arranging this debate. I have great respect for my fellow debater. Gloria has tried to make some excellent points. I emphasize the word 'tried.' I don't use that word negatively. I use it to emphasize my position. In the five minutes allotted Gloria, she spent half the time dealing with the challenges of her speech. I have empathy for that challenge—it's certainly not her fault. But by the time the bell rang, her argument was incomplete. She was unable to articulate her full case. We don't even know the extent of her full case. Ironically, though, by failing to complete her argument, she has already made my case.

"Every debate that Bloom Middle School will enter this year will be timed. According to the rule book, there are no provisions for extra time for any reason. Consequently, I agree with Gloria that the proposition that Mr. Talbot introduced—'As a member of a debate team, should a person who stutters be given special consideration?'—is not relevant. It's not relevant because even if we agree that a person who stutters should be given special consideration, it is not within our jurisdiction to grant that consideration. The rules of middle school and high school debates are outside of our influence. And so, if Gloria were on our team, we would unfairly suffer because of her inability to effectively debate within the time allotted."

As Mack takes his seat, his buddies cheer. I feel sick to my stomach. When Mr. Talbot speaks, I feel even sicker. This is so unfair to Gloria.

"Gloria," he says, "I want you to know that we value you and always want you with us as a researcher whenever we enter debate tournaments. No one does a better job of researching complicated issues than you. But Mack has made his point. You are unable to make your case in the allotted time, and this makes you a liability in a tournament. You can research, but you should not be a speaker. I think most of you will agree with my decision."

"I don't!" I yell from the back of the room.

Everyone turns to look at me. I know they think I'm only on her side because I'm also a person who stutters. That might be partially true. I know how frustrating it is to have a good point to make and not be given a chance to make it.

"Debate is based on disagreement," says Mr. Talbot. "Ideally, though, we can disagree without being disagreeable."

I want to stand up and say, *Well, I don't agree, and I don't feel like being agreeable. Sometimes a person needs to be disagreeable to make their case. You can speak politely all you want about denying my friend her chance to debate, but that doesn't make it any more agreeable to me.*

But I don't say anything, because the debate is over and the kids are leaving. The auditorium empties out quickly. Everyone is patting Mack on the back, congratulating him for a job well done. Gloria is still sitting in her seat up at the front. Chuck and I go up to her. She is not crying, but I can see the anger and frustration in her eyes. I don't know what to say to her. She's not going to be allowed to debate, and that sucks.

After school, Chuck, Gloria, and I walk over to Rubato's, one of our favorite hangouts. It's an amazing little bakery owned by the parents of my friend Gino. The Rubatos originally came from Italy, and their small shop is decorated with colorful posters of Rome, Florence, and Venice. We always get lemonade, which is our favorite—for some reason it's better at Rubato's than any other place. Chuck orders two doughnuts with sprinkles, and I get my usual vanilla cupcake. Gloria is still too upset to eat.

We sit at a table in the corner. Even though it's September, it feels like June. It's eighty-five degrees and humid. I offer Gloria a bite of my cupcake, but she refuses. Then Amia shows up, and Gloria's mood changes. Gloria met Amia before school started since she lives nearby, and they became friends right away. Amia is still in their warm-up suit from track practice. Amia is seriously fast. I tried to race them in a two hundred meters run once, just for fun. I'll never make that mistake again.

"Glo! How'd your debate go?"

"N-n-n-n-not good," Gloria says.

Gloria tells Amia what happened in debate.

"That's not right," Amia says.

"I know, it's so unfair."

"This school really needs to change." Amia shakes their head and puts an arm around Gloria.

"That's why I want Jayson to r-r-r-run for president,"

Gloria says, looking at me.

"That's an awesome idea!" Amia exclaims. "We have to come up with the perfect campaign slogan. Maybe 'Let Linden lead!'"

"Or 'Vote for Jay! He knows the way!'" Gloria offers.

"W-w-w-wait just a second," I object.

"'Don't ruin our day, son. Vote for Jayson,'" Chuck says, laughing. They're all cracking each other up, but I'm not so sure. I've been going back and forth about running since Gloria first brought it up. I feel like the real race is me versus my stutter. It's only a matter of time before I'm defeated.

"Look," I say, "we know that the school officers are just do-nothing p-p-p-positions. They're head of the student council, but the council is a joke. I heard that last year the council's big c-c-c-c-contribution was to buy the cheerleaders fancier uniforms."

"That's even more reason to run," says Gloria. "You can m-m-m-m-make the council do something that m-m-m-m-matters."

"What Mack d-d-d-d-did to you back in that class really did make me mad," I say, "but I have another idea."

"What's that?" asks Gloria.

"Y-y-y-you run."

"I'd n-n-n-n-never win," she says.

"Neither would I."

"You have a better chance than m-m-m-me," says Gloria.

"Why?" I ask.

"I'm n-n-n-n-not as popular as you. I'm still n-n-n-new, and I've already m-m-m-made some enemies. I'm too d-d-d-d-direct with everyone. Sometimes I hurt people's f-f-f-feelings when I don't mean to. B-b-b-b-besides, there are more boys in our class than girls. And boys always vote for other boys."

"Gloria has a point, Jayson," says Chuck. "I think you've got a good chance."

"See that," says Gloria. "And Chuck's being objective."

"L-l-l-let's get real here," I say. "Against Mack Gaines? Do I really have any chance at all?"

"It's not a m-m-m-m-matter of chance," says Gloria. "It's a matter of planning. We need to p-p-p-plan a campaign. A campaign b-b-b-based on the issues that matter."

"A campaign is just a popularity c-c-c-contest," I say.

"Well, that's what we're going to ch-ch-ch-ch-change," says Gloria. "Issues are going to make all the difference."

"But what are the issues?" I ask.

"Well, you were just talking about one of them, Jayson," Amia says. "Students need to be heard. Class president and student council need to be more than just honorary positions.

They need to give us a voice."

"That's true," Chuck says. "How many times have we heard that we can't change something in the past week alone? Coach Croft's decision about the size of the team, the rules of the debate team . . ."

"Gender-inclusive bathrooms!" says Amia. "I've been trying to talk to Principal Goodman about it since our first year. He keeps brushing me off, telling me that's up to the school board, that he can't do anything about it. He acted like I couldn't possibly be serious."

"G-g-g-giving students a v-v-v-voice," says Gloria. "It covers so m-m-m-much. P-p-p-probably things we d-d-d-don't even know about yet. What do you think, Jayson?"

"I think it's a great idea," I say.

"Goodman is going to hate it," says Chuck.

"That's even more reason we n-n-need to do it," says Gloria.

"But do you really agree with it?" Amia asks me. "You have to be sincere about it."

"I absolutely positively agree," I say. "It's the right thing to do, and there's something else I'm s-s-s-sure about. I'm sure that Gloria should run for vice president. In debate class, she was discriminated against. We can t-t-talk about that in the campaign."

Amia jumps up again and screams, "Yes! We have some really important issues and two cool candidates."

"Two people who s-s-s-s-stutter on the same ticket?" asks Gloria.

"It's unusual," says Chuck.

"And unpredictable," adds Amia.

"Unpredictable is a good thing," I say, remembering the excitement of a mild drizzle turning into a major thunderstorm.

"Well, then it's decided," says Amia.

"I-i-it's a good thing. W-w-we have to hand in the forms to declare candidacy tomorrow."

After our discussion, my head is spinning. Things are moving fast, but I'm feeling good about the way they're moving. They're moving in a positive direction.

Amia and Gloria decide to take a bike ride, and Chuck and I head to a playground for a pickup basketball game. Hoop will help get our minds off all the other stuff. Pickup games are fun, and this one, with some older guys we've never met before, is super competitive. Our team loses, but Chuck and I don't really care. We just love the game, and it's the best feeling in the world to be playing with my favorite teammate again.

CHAPTER 12

Steph Curry vs. Jayson Tatum

I had planned to tell Dad about my final decision to run for class president after school, but we had tickets to go to the Golden State Warriors–Boston Celtics game with Dr. Dan. I'm not stoked to see Dr. Dan, especially after I had such a great session with Dr. Fine, but I'd never pass up the chance to see my favorite team. I decide to postpone telling Dad until after the game. If I tell him before the game, he'll probably tell Dr. Dan. That's a discussion I want to avoid. I just want to concentrate on basketball and watching my favorite team win.

It's nice to clear my mind for a little while. I slip on my

Steph Curry jersey, grab my Warriors cap, throw on some jeans, and am ready to roll. Dr. Dan pulls up in his black BMW, and he, Dad, and I make the forty-five-minute drive over the bridge to the Chase Center in the Mission District of downtown San Francisco.

The arena is jammed with 18,000 fans. I wonder where our seats will be. Dr. Dan has season tickets, but how close to the floor? It turns out, very close. They're in the third row at midcourt! Of course, I'll be rooting for the Golden State Warriors, but I'm also a secret fan of Jayson Tatum because not only do we share a name, we spell it the same way. As we take our seats, the players are warming up.

"You can go ahead and walk down to the edge of the court," says Dr. Dan.

Wow! That's just what I do. I'm close enough to shake Steph Curry's hand. At one point, Jayson Tatum comes over to whisper something in Curry's ear. I'm two feet away but can't hear what he says. They smile and bump fists. Friendly rivals. I wonder if Mack and I can ever be friendly rivals like that? At the moment, it doesn't seem like it. Unfriendly rivals is more like it.

When the buzzer sounds to start the first quarter, I rush back up to my seat. I'm glad that Dad, rather than me, is in the middle seat. I really don't want to be next to Dr. Dan and worry about thinking of things to say. I just want to concentrate on the game.

Unfortunately, the game is lopsided from the start. The Celtics are crushing us. Curry is having an off night, and Tatum can't be stopped. I can't cheer when Tatum keeps hitting threes—after all, he's our opponent—but I'm still excited for him. He plays with such smooth confidence. After Curry, he's definitely my favorite NBA star.

Because the game isn't close, Dad and Dr. Dan spend most of their time chatting about some of the women they knew in college. Only because Dad told me, I know that Dr. Dan is divorced and never had children. Back when I was ten, Dad had a woman friend named Augusta. Once in a while, she came over for dinner. She was nice enough, but it turned out she was allergic to dogs. Even though I put Caitin in the yard, Augusta didn't make it through dessert. Later, she and Dad broke up. I never asked why, but I was glad. I've never been comfortable with Dad dating women. I like things how they are, just the two of us and Caitin.

At halftime, I'm looking around, when I suddenly see three people stand up from their courtside seats. It's Mack and Suzy, with Suzy's mom. As they turn around, I don't want them to see me. I want to duck. But I'm too late. They see me and wave. And then—*oh no!*—they walk up the rows to say hello. That means I'll have to introduce them to Dad and Dr. Dan.

"Hey, Jayson," says Mack. "Great to see you, man. Hope we come back the second half."

"M-m-m-m-m-me too."

"Hi, Ian," Suzy's mother says to my dad. She leans in and gives him a kiss on the cheek.

How does she know my dad?

"Hi," my dad says, looking at me out of the corner of his eye.

Dad introduces Dr. Dan. Everyone shakes hands.

"Good meeting you, Mr. Lowe," says Mack.

"Dr. Lowe," Dad corrects him.

"Sorry," says Mack. "Dr. Lowe. What kind of medicine do you practice?"

That's the last question I want to hear.

"I'm a speech pathologist," Dr. Dan answers.

Both Mack and Suzy nod. They don't say, *Oh, of course. We understand. You're the kind of doctor Jayson really needs,* but I hear them thinking it. Plus, I hate the word "pathologist." It's close to "pathetic," which is what they probably think I am. Why can't Dr. Dan have simply said, *I'm a therapist.* The whole thing makes me mad at everyone.

"You have nice friends, Jayson," says Dr. Dan.

I want to say, *They're not my friends*, but I just nod.

"Mack, Jayson tells me you're running for class president," Dad says.

"So, have you decided . . . ?" Dr. Dan starts to ask me.

"Yes. I'm running too," I say quickly. I hadn't planned on saying it, but now here we are.

"You are?" Mack asks. He exchanges a confused look with Suzy.

I respond firmly. "I am. And Gloria is r-r-r-running for vice president. And we're putting in our names tomorrow."

"Laura told me that Suzy is also running for vice president, with Mack," Dad says.

"L-L-Laura?" I've already guessed who Laura is, but I'm not planning on making it easy for my dad.

"Suzy's mom."

"S-s-s-since when are you so close?" I ask.

"We're not 'so close,' Jayson. We've just recently become friends."

I remember hearing that Suzy had a single mom, but I don't really want to hear anything more about her friendship with Dad.

"This will be fun, Jayson," Mack says with a smirk. "May the best team win."

We are for sure still unfriendly rivals.

Just then, the buzzer sounds for the start of the second half, and Mack, Suzy, and Suzy's mom go back to their seats. In the third quarter, Golden State comes as close as ten points. But in the fourth quarter, Jayson Tatum goes off and ends the night scoring forty-eight points, making me happy for him and sad for my Warriors. It's the cherry on top of my messed-up sundae of an evening.

Sitting in the back of Dr. Dan's BMW, the ride home is quiet. I look at the lights on the long Bay Bridge, the tall buildings of downtown Oakland, the sight of the old Coliseum Arena, where the Warriors used to play, the hills and the highway that lead to Bloom. My mind is working overtime. I'm not happy that I told Dad my decision to run in the middle of a basketball game, especially with Dr. Dan sitting there. I'm also not happy about seeing Mack and Suzy and learning about Dad and Suzy's mom. Can he be serious? Why didn't he tell me about her? I want to know what's going on, but I don't want to talk about it in front of Dr. Dan.

Dr. Dan drops us off at home and we thank him for the tickets. Inside, I open my mouth to ask Dad about Laura Best, but then he says, "I've invited Laura for dinner this Saturday night. I'd like for her to get to know you."

"Are you two d-d-dating?" I ask, trying not to get upset.

"I was going to mention it to you, Jayson, but I didn't want to be premature."

"Wh-wh-wh-what does that mean?"

"It means we're just getting to know each other. We've seen each other a couple of times. I didn't want to make it seem . . . too . . . important." Dad says, rubbing the back of his head awkwardly.

"Her d-d-d-daughter goes to my school. D-d-d-didn't you think I'd find out?"

"I just said that I was going to mention it."

"But you didn't," I say.

"Well, I just did, son."

"I bet Suzy doesn't like the idea."

"Why do you say that?"

"Because Suzy is Mack's girlfriend. And Mack d-d-d-d-doesn't like me. And now Gloria is running against Suzy for vice president. Of all people, Dad . . ."

"Jayson, I think you're making a big deal out of nothing."

"This is a big deal, Dad. We have serious changes we w-w-want to make at school."

"You don't think you're being too hasty?" he asks.

My heart is beating fast.

"Why?"

"Well, you had told me that Dan felt it was better to wait

till next year when your fluency . . ."

"I d-d-d-d-don't care about that. I d-d-d-don't care what Dr. Dan says. Dr. Fine says stuttering is something to accept, not to f-f-fight."

"I just don't want to see you get hurt. Self-esteem . . ."

"It s-s-s-seems like you're s-s-s-sure I'm g-g-g-g-g-going to lose."

"You're twisting my words, Jayson. Of course, I think you'll win. And of course you should make your own decision about whether to run. It's only that . . ."

"Only what, Dad?"

"Maybe you're right. Maybe it is time to go to bed, son. After a good night's sleep, our heads will be clear and we can discuss it in the morning."

In the morning, we don't discuss anything. During breakfast, we hardly say a word. It's the first real fight we've had in a long time.

CHAPTER 13

Declaration Day

With our forms and recommendations in hand, Gloria and I walk into Principal Goodman's office. He's sitting behind his large wooden desk, and he seems surprised to see us. It's hard to miss it when Principal Goodman is surprised. He has big bushy eyebrows that are just a little too expressive. They race up toward his curly hair like a couple of scared caterpillars looking for shelter.

"I w-w-w-w-want to run for president," I say.

"And I w-w-w-w-want to run for v-v-v-vice president," says Gloria.

He stares at us for moment, and then his caterpillars tilt

toward each other in confusion.

"I presumed this election would be uncontested," he says slowly. "These elections usually are." He seems annoyed that we've made things more complicated than usual.

We just shrug and hand him our paperwork.

After seeing that our letters of recommendation are legit, he asks, "Are you certain you want to run? You are aware that Mack Gaines and Suzy Best are already nominated?"

We both nod.

"Well," he says, "good luck to both of you, then."

He's not very convincing.

Gloria and I meet Chuck and Amia in the cafeteria. Preeda joins us along with Gino. Preeda was a new student last year when her family moved here from Thailand, and she, Gino, Chuck, and I all became friends in Mrs. Presto's seventh-grade science class.

"So you're challenging the Mack machine," says Gino.

"OMG. I can't wait," exclaims Preeda. "Mack is going down. I'm so sick of having decisions made before anyone even talks about them," she says. "Usually by someone close to the mayor—like his son!"

It's funny. For most of my time in middle school, I thought I was the only one besides Chuck who wasn't in the

Mack Gaines Fan Club. In the few days I've decided to run against him, I've met so many more. And it's not just Mack that everyone seems to want to change, it's all the stuff at the school that goes on that people don't talk about. Amia was the first person I heard talk about the gender-inclusive bathrooms, but since they mentioned it, two other students have brought it up to me. I wonder how much more I will learn about other students before the election is over.

Just then, Principal Goodman's voice comes over the loudspeaker.

"Attention, Bloom Bobcats. Nominations have been received for class president and vice president. Elections will be held the Wednesday before Thanksgiving. For eighth-grade vice president, candidates are Suzy Best and Gloria Lopez."

The students are surprised to hear another name other than Suzy's. Spontaneously, a shout goes up: "Suzy! Suzy! Suzy! Suzy! Suzy!"

I look over at Gloria. She's not smiling.

"And for president," Principal Goodman continues, "there are also two candidates. Mack Gaines and Jayson Linden."

An even louder and longer shout goes up. "Mack! Mack! Mack! Mack! Mack! Mack!"

Mack, Suzy, and a bunch of their basketball and cheer-leader friends are sitting at the popular kids' table on the other side of the lunchroom. Most of the noise is coming from that side.

"Remember a lot of their supporters are cheerleaders," Gino says. "They know how to be loud."

The kids don't stop shouting until Mack and Suzy stand up. They wave like they're the king and queen of England. They also wave across the room at me and Gloria. Maybe they're just being polite. But I don't take it that way. I take it as taunting.

When I get home from practice, Dad is there. There's still leftover tension between us.

"Hey, Jayson, I picked up some lasagna. You feel like a little lasagna tonight?"

"Sure." Lasagna's my second-favorite meal after Al's burgers.

"How was school?" he asks.

"Good. Gloria and I announced that we're r-r-r-running."

"Great! Are there any other candidates besides Mack and Suzy?"

"Nope."

"Well, that makes things simpler. Are you working up a platform?"

"We are. There's a lot of important s-s-s-stuff we want to change."

"I want to hear about it, but first I want to say that if you're uncomfortable with Laura coming for dinner Saturday, I can cancel it."

"You don't have to d-d-d-do that, Dad. You can invite anyone over you want to. It's y-y-your house."

"It's *our* house, Jayson. You know you're always welcome to have your friends here."

"Could I invite a f-f-f-friend over Saturday night as well?"

"Of course. Invite whoever you like. There'll be enough food for everyone."

When Saturday arrives, I'm nervous. I'm not sure how all this will go. I've never really talked to Laura Best. I mean, sure, I've seen her around, picking up Suzy, and at basketball games, but only from a distance. The first time I ever talked to her was at the Warriors-Celtics game, and that wasn't exactly a conversation, more of just a quick hello. When the doorbell rings, Dad's out in the yard grilling steak. So I answer the door.

"Hi, Jayson," says Mrs. Best, as if she knows me.

"C-c-c-come on in, Mrs. Best."

"Call me Laura, please," she says, stepping inside.

That won't be easy, so I don't say anything. She's pretty. Very pretty. Pretty like her daughter. Pretty blond hair, pretty smile, pretty blue pantsuit. She also seems a little cold. I feel like she's being nice to me because she has to, not because she wants to. She's carrying a bottle of white wine with a big white bow on it.

"I've been so eager to see your house," she says as she looks around. "Your dad said the house was modest, but I had a feeling it'd be beautiful. And it certainly is. He has such wonderful taste. I see he's out there in the yard."

"He's g-g-g-g-grilling," I say.

"Excuse me while I go tell him hello," she says, eager to get past me and get to Dad.

I watch Mrs. Best open the sliding glass door and greet Dad with a kiss on his cheek. He gives her a hug. I'm really uncomfortable.

I've already set the table and filled the pitcher with water.

Dad comes in to get a couple of wineglasses.

"When is Chuck getting here?" he asks.

"I asked G-G-G-Gloria to come over since Chuck is busy with his family today."

"Really?" He looks surprised.

"You said I c-c-c-c-could invite whoever I w-w-w-w-want, Dad."

"You've been hanging out with her a lot."

"I don't want to talk about that. Especially n-n-n-n-not now," I say, looking out at Laura in the dining room.

Dad laughs. "It'll be good to see Gloria and get to know her better."

Gloria and I had decided to get together and talk about ideas for the campaign this weekend anyway. She'd invited me to her house, but then, when Chuck couldn't come to the dinner with Mrs. Best, I got the idea of inviting Gloria. I told her that Suzy's mom would be there, but she didn't seem to mind. She thought it was funny that my dad was dating Mrs. Best.

The doorbell rings, and it's Gloria. Caitin is the first to greet her. She's about the friendliest dog in the world.

"Dad and Mrs. Best, this is my friend Gloria," I say as we walk into the kitchen together.

"Nice to meet you, Gloria," Dad says, shaking her hand. "I hope you're hungry, because it's time to eat!"

"Awesome, I'm starving!" Gloria says.

Dad brings all the food over to the kitchen table, and we all sit down, Dad and Mrs. Best on one side of the table,

Gloria and I on the other. Mrs. Best knows that Gloria is running for class vice president against her daughter and that I'm running for president against her daughter's boyfriend. I'm just hoping the subject won't come up. Luckily, Mrs. Best has so much to say about herself, it seems like we might be safe. She dominates the dinner conversation. It's hard for anyone to get a word in. She talks about how she loves going into San Francisco to hear the symphony orchestra. . . .

"You simply *must* come with me sometime, Ian. They did the most transcendent performance. . . ."

She spends the next fifty minutes talking about some composer no one has ever heard of or cares about. Then she moves on to painters. But the whole time she's not really talking about composers or painters, she's talking about herself. The first time *she* went to the symphony. The art history class *she* took. Dad seems to be tricked, though, because she brings up Renoir, Goya, and some of his other favorite artists. Gloria and I try not to roll our eyes. Then Mrs. Best complains/brags about all the work she has ahead of her on the board of the Bloom Historical Society to help save several landmark buildings from being destroyed.

"There's talk of tearing down the current middle school for a more modern building," she says. "I'm opposed. I'm sure you're opposed as well, Ian. The current school is a prime example of mid-century architecture that needs to be preserved."

"Our c-c-c-c-current school is really in bad shape," says Gloria. "It was originally built as a private all-boys school, so there aren't e-e-e-e-enough girls' bathrooms. And that doesn't take into consideration our nonbinary students. I think it's a good idea to redo the bathrooms and make them gender neutral."

"Oh," says Mrs. Best.

I can tell she doesn't like the idea.

"Won't that involve considerable expense?" she asks.

"It just means t-t-t-taking out the urinals and putting private stalls in all the bathrooms," I say. "That sh-sh-sh-shouldn't cost too much."

"But there are other things to consider," says Mrs. Best.

"The good thing is that it will make everyone f-f-f-f-feel included," says Gloria.

"Is that part of your campaign platform?" asks Dad.

Just when I thought we were safe from any campaign talk.

"Are you still planning on running?" asks Mrs. Best.

Here we go.

Mrs. Best looks flustered. "Suzy didn't think that you and Jayson were serious about running."

"That's what everyone thought," says Gloria, "but everyone was wr-wr-wr-wr-wr-wrong."

No one talks—and it's not a comfortable silence. I take a bite of steak, and the squeak of my teeth against the meat seems deafening. Dad digs into his baked potato. Mrs. Best sips her wine. Gloria finishes off her glass of ginger ale. Other than "Good steak" and "This wine is really nice," nothing more is said.

After dinner, Dad and Mrs. Best sit in the den and talk while Gloria and I go out in the yard to talk about the campaign and how to get more kids on our side. Caitin comes with us. We make a list of ideas and possible slogans, but eventually we can't help but bring up the obvious.

"I c-c-can't believe your dad is dating—"

"I know!" Normally I try not to interrupt people—I get sick of everyone doing it to me. But I just couldn't stand to hear her finish her sentence. I didn't want to hear "dating Mrs. Best." Maybe if we didn't say it, it wouldn't be true.

"I-i-if I had to hear about one m-more committee or board that she was part of . . ." Gloria says. "S-s-s-suddenly I almost f-feel bad for S-S-Suzy."

"Let's forget about her," I say. "We have a campaign to plan."

For the rest of the evening, Gloria and I talk about the

election and we have a lot of good ideas, but I'm starting to get even more nervous. At nine thirty, Mrs. Best comes outside to tell us good night. I'm glad she's leaving. I have a feeling she is too. A little later, when Dad volunteers to drive Gloria home, I come along for the ride. Dad has the classical station on the radio.

"Would you kids rather hear something else?" he asks.

"Yes," I say, with my finger already on the button for a pop hits station. Bruno Mars comes on.

As the music plays, we stay silent. I poke my head out the window and look up at the night sky. I'm feeling confused about Dad dating Mrs. Best. I'm also feeling afraid that Gloria and I are about to get into something over our heads. But the sight of the Milky Way calms me down.

After we drop off Gloria, Dad asks, "Is there anything you'd like to discuss?"

I say, "Not really. If you want to listen to your classical music, go ahead."

Dad switches the station, and a symphony comes on. I'm not crazy about classical music, but at this moment, I don't mind it. I'm happy Dad doesn't start a discussion I don't want to have.

CHAPTER 14

Food Fight!

Monday's not my favorite day of the week. It means five days of school and five nights of homework are ahead of me. But Monday lunch is always fun because I get to catch up with my friends, and we have a lot to discuss regarding the campaign.

The lunchroom is loud as usual. I'm sitting with Gloria, Chuck, Gino, Preeda, and Amia. We've just started eating when Mack walks by and asks Gino, "Hey, are you part of the stutterers club now?"

Preeda glares at Mack, and Gino bunches his fists

together, jumping up from the table.

"What did you just say?" Gino yells.

"You heard what I said," Mack shouts back, giving Gino a shove.

Amia takes a handful of tuna salad and mushes it against Mack's face. Preeda starts laughing, and two of Suzy's friends start squirting her with bottles of ketchup. Gloria takes her piece of banana cream pie and flings it at one of the ketchup squirters. Bull's-eye! Other kids, who have nothing to do with either side, start throwing burgers and hot dogs. Someone screams, "Food fight!" Before I know it, I have a face full of mayonnaise. Chuck stands up to throw his sandwich and slips in a trail of pudding. I try to catch him but get pulled down to the floor. Somehow Preeda ends up there with us. It's a full-on food fight.

Our school has only two security guards. They both come running into the lunchroom. They do their best to break up the fighting, but by then, things are out of control. As I duck a milk carton being thrown in my direction, I glance over to the other side of the lunchroom and see that Mack has jumped on top of a table. It's no surprise that he's taken this opportunity to be the center of attention and play the hero. He helps Suzy onto the table so she can stand next to him. She has pudding in her hair.

He lifts up both his hands and shouts, "Stop! Everyone just stop!"

Suzy echoes him. "This isn't right!"

Somehow, everyone stops.

Minutes later, Principal Goodman arrives. None of the teachers on lunch duty or the security guards have seen who started it. The first students the principal approaches are Mack and Suzy, who are still standing on the table. They step down and confer with Mr. Goodman for several minutes. Afterward, the principal walks over to where Amia and Gloria are looking for napkins to wipe food off their faces.

"Come with me, you two," he says to Amia and Gloria.

"What?" I loudly protest. "Why? They didn't s-s-s-s-start it. Mack did."

"That's enough!" Principal Goodman barks. "Another word out of you and you'll be coming along as well."

"Good!" I shout. "I w-w-w-w-w-w-want to come along. I want you to know what r-r-r-r-really happened."

Principal Goodman also asks Mack and Suzy to come to his office. He already sees them as the good guys, the peacemakers. I'm furious.

The five of us walk to the principal's office. Amia and Gloria are given paper towels to clean off their faces. Though there's a couch and a couple of chairs, the only one seated is Mr. Goodman. He sits in his high-back chair like a judge in a courtroom.

"From what I hear, Amia," he says, "you began this fight."

"It was a food fight," I say.

"But there was physical violence," he says.

"If y-y-y-you call getting a little p-p-p-pudding in your eye v-v-v-violence," I say.

"And that's something you approve of, Jayson?"

"No. It's just s-s-s-s-something that happened. And it happened because—"

"I didn't have anything to do with it," says Mack.

"Mack had everything to d-d-d-d-do with it," I say. "He s-s-s-s-said something n-n-n-nasty to Preeda and Gino about people who s-s-stutter. About m-m-m-me and Gloria."

"I saw Amia push food in Mack's face," says Suzy.

"That happened l-l-l-later," says Gloria.

"Mack made fun of Jayson and Gloria," says Amia.

"I've heard enough," says Principal Goodman. "I'm going to suspend Amia and Gloria for three school days. I don't care what your reasons are—you can't incite violence here."

"B-b-b-b-b-but it's fine to be a b-b-b-bully, I s-s-s-s-s-suppose," I say. "Amia and Gloria didn't d-d-d-do anything wrong. I h-hope you're proud of y-y-y-yourself, Mack."

"Keep up this back talk, Jayson," says the principal, "and I'll be forced to suspend you as well."

"I s-s-s-s-suspend m-m-m-myself!" I say. "In s-s-s-s-solidarity!"

"Done," Principal Goodman declares. "Meeting over."

When I get home, I find out that Dad has already been called by Principal Goodman.

"This sounds serious, Jayson." Dad frowns.

"It is s-s-s-s-seriously stupid."

"I agree. Getting suspended isn't a smart move."

"It was for absolutely no r-r-r-r-reason."

"According to Mr. Goodman, there was a fight—"

"It was a food fight! P-p-p-people w-w-were throwing pudding, not bricks!"

"Okay, but you were in the middle of it. And apparently so was your friend Gloria."

"Is that what Suzy's m-m-m-m-mother told you?"

"I haven't spoken to Laura."

"I'm sure you w-w-w-w-will."

"Jayson . . ."

There's nothing left to say. I turn away from my father and go to my room with Caitin.

CHAPTER 15

The Bloom Squad

Three of us are suspended for three days—Gloria, Amia, and me. Chuck, Preeda, and Gino also decide to stay out of school in protest.

During our suspension we all meet up for lunch on Thursday at Rock 'N Bowl. We're sitting at a big booth while Big Al takes our order.

"You guys look like you're about to cause some trouble," he says.

"Maybe," says Chuck, "but only the good kind."

Al nods approvingly. "You got your own little Bloom squad from the looks of it."

"I like that," says Chuck. "Now the Bloom Squad needs to say something."

"We need to m-m-m-m-make a st-st-statement," says Gloria.

"A resolution," Chuck says.

"A declaration," says Preeda. "Jayson? Wanna write it?"

"Why m-m-m-m-m-me?" I ask.

"Because you like to write," says Chuck. "And it will be good for your campaign. People know you stand for something. It's a good place to lay out everything you want to address in your campaign."

"We'll all be in it together," says Amia. "A declaration from the Bloom Squad."

"What are we declaring?" asks Preeda.

"The right to be heard," Chuck says.

"Yes!" Amia shouts while Big Al flips the burgers and salts the fries.

"It will turn the tables on Goodman," says Preeda. "And it will show that we're not afraid of saying what we believe."

"Preeda's right," Chuck agrees. "It's like the unofficial start of the campaign."

"To get everyone involved," says Gloria, "maybe the b-b-b-best thing to do is make lots of copies of the statement and get the k-k-k-k-kids to sign. That way we'll have a big stack to plop d-d-d-d-down on the principal's desk."

"We can make copies for free at my parents' place," says Preeda. Her parents own a shipping service store with copy machines.

"Perfect!" says Gino.

Big Al serves up the burgers with cheese melting off the sides. We stop talking and dig in.

By the end of the afternoon, with the six of us sitting around the booth and me typing on my iPad, we come up with the following.

DECLARATION OF THE RIGHT TO BE HEARD

We, the students and citizens of Bloom Middle School, hereby declare that it is our right as members of a community to have our voices heard.

We should be heard in forums that affect our future and the future of our community.

In hearings where cases are being made against us, we should be present and allowed to defend ourselves.

We should also be allowed to speak in any place where thoughts, ideas, or opinions are influencing our environment.

In short, we should be allowed to speak in any situation that affects us and our community.

"Well, that's simple enough," says Chuck.

"That's the whole p-p-p-p-point," I say. "Keep it short and simple. It only takes ten seconds to read. That gives us a better chance to get lots of signatures. We'll print it up and hand it out at school so people can sign it and then give it back to us to present to Principal Goodman. The more sig-natures we can get, the better."

"Principal Goodman is going to be furious," says Gino.

"G-g-g-g-good," says Gloria.

"This could g-g-g-g-get us in more trouble," I say.

"Oh well," says Amia.

"He could stop you and Jayson from running for class president and vice president," says Preeda.

"He wouldn't dare," says Amia.

"I'm not so sure," adds Chuck.

"I say we go for it," Amia insists.

So we do.

The first day we are allowed to return to school, Dad drives me so I can get there a little early. I read the declaration to him on the way.

"This is a big risk for you, Jayson," he says. "Are you sure you want to start your campaign this way?"

"I've n-n-n-never been m-m-m-more sure. M-m-m-my friends and I are in it t-t-t-t-together."

"Well, I'm nervous for you. But I have to admit I'm proud too."

He pats me on the shoulder. "Have a good day, Jayson."

"Thanks, Dad." I get out of the car and head into the building.

My friends and I distribute flyers with our declaration all over school before the morning bell rings. Bloom has eight hundred students—over two hundred in each grade. We want to get as many kids as possible to sign the declaration and give it back to us before we present it to Principal Goodman. We stand by all the school entrances and hand it out to everyone.

I'm happy when students ask me and Gloria if this is about our running for president and vice president. We tell them it's just a general protest but, yes, it's all about standing up to something we think is wrong. Some kids seem excited by that. Others just shrug. We don't try to talk anyone into signing. If they have questions, we answer them.

A few friends of Mack and Suzy take a declaration and, right in front of us, tear it up. We don't give them the satisfaction of reacting. Other kids congratulate us for having the guts to make this protest.

At the end of the day, we quickly count the number of signed documents. It's over a hundred! We're really happy and hurry over to the principal's office and hand him the thick stack of signed copies.

He reads it quickly and scowls.

"I presume, Jayson, that this is your doing."

"It's f-f-f-f-from everyone who signed."

"But you wrote it, right?"

"It was done by all of us h-h-h-here." I point to my friends.

"But what is the point of this declaration, Jayson? You've already been reinstated in school. The punishment is over."

"The point of the d-d-d-d-d-declaration, Principal Goodman, is to say that we d-d-d-deserve to have a say about wh-wh-wh-what happens in our school. The declaration s-s-s-speaks for itself."

"But to what purpose? Do you think this makes you a leader? Is it a part of your campaign?"

"We never m-m-m-mention the campaign," I say.

"You're telling me that it doesn't draw attention to you?"

"No, s-s-s-s-sir, it doesn't. I'm j-j-j-j-just one of a hundred kids who signed it."

"But you're the one handing it out."

"Not th-th-the only one."

"But the main one."

"I wouldn't s-s-s-say that."

"What *would* you say, young man?"

"I would s-s-s-say that the declaration is an expression of f-f-f-free speech."

"And defiance."

"Part of f-f-f-f-free speech is that you get to be d-d-d-defiant. In f-f-fact. Maybe that's th-th-the p-p-p—"

"You do understand, Jayson," he interrupts. "That I can take even stronger measures."

"Yes, sir, I d-d-d-d-do."

"As of now, I've decided to drop the matter. It's already

received more attention than it deserves. The incident has embarrassed this school. The sooner it is forgotten, the better. You may leave."

My first thought is *Victory!* We did what we set out to do. We let the school know that Principal Goodman has been unfair. Because he's afraid of publicity—that maybe the local *Bloom Daily Chronicle* will pick up the story—he isn't going to respond. And without any response, that means our declaration will stand.

CHAPTER 16

Big Decision

By midweek, most kids at school have read the declaration and like that we've stood up to the principal and made our point. That makes me feel great. Surprisingly, it's even printed in the school paper, despite Mack's friend Sam being the editor. Even though mostly everyone has already read it at that point, it's nice to have it in an "official" student forum. As we're getting ready to go to Rubato's to celebrate, I get a text from Dad reminding me I have my appointment with Dr. Dan. I'm not thrilled about it, but I promised Dad I would go.

I decide to start the session by telling Dr. Dan the details of the food fight and then showing him a copy of the declaration.

"Is this something you wrote for school?" he asks. "You've never shown me any of your schoolwork. I'm happy to read it."

After he reads it, he doesn't seem so happy. In fact, it's hard to tell how he feels about it.

"Is this something to help you in your campaign to become president?" he asks.

"That's what the p-p-p-p-p-p-principal w-w-w-w-wanted to know."

"And what did you tell him?"

"The s-s-s-s-s-same thing I'll t-t-t-t-t-tell you, Dr. Dan. It's a general p-p-p-p-p-protest."

"How does your father feel about it?"

"Dad's proud of me. But how do you f-f-f-f-f-feel about it, Dr. Dan? Doesn't what h-h-h-h-h-happened to us m-m-m-m-make y-y-y-y-y-y-y-you angry?"

"That's not my role. I'm your speech therapist, and in that role, I have to say that your fluency has taken a step back. You seem to be stuttering more than ever. Why do think that is?"

"Because I'm a-a-a-a-a-a-angry."

"Anger doesn't have to hamper your fluency."

"But if it d-d-d-does, s-s-s-s-s-so what?"

"You seem angry at me, Jayson."

"I d-d-d-d-d-don't f-f-f-f-f-f-f-feel like you're behind me."

"I'm sorry you feel that way. I'm one of your biggest supporters."

I take a big gulp. I know what I want to say, but I'm not sure if I can say it. I need to build up my nerve. I take another big gulp, and after ten or twenty seconds, I finally say, "If you don't mind, Dr. D-D-D-D-Dan, I think I'd like to leave now."

"But we have another forty minutes."

"Y-y-y-y-yes, I kn-kn-know."

"I think that would be unwise."

"Since my s-s-s-s-speech is g-g-g-g-g-getting worse, I think it'd b-b-b-b-be unwise to s-s-s-s-stay."

"You've never acted this way in here before."

"I just w-w-w-w-w-w-w-w-w-w-want to l-l-l-l-l-l-l-l-l-l-l-leave."

"We've spent years working together, Jayson. I suggest you think this over carefully."

I don't respond. I just get up and leave.

By the time I get home, Dr. Dan has already called Dad.

"He said you ran out of the session, Jayson."

"I w-w-w-w-w-walked out."

"Why?"

"I d-d-d-d-don't think Dr. D-D-D-D-Dan is helping me."

"Because your speech is getting worse?"

"Because . . . I . . . I d-d-d-d-don't know why . . ."

"This thing at school has upset you, Jayson. That's even more reason for you to get the support you need."

"Dr. Dan isn't g-g-g-g-g-giving me support. He just m-m-m-m-m-makes me feel bad for stuttering so much, and that makes me st-st-st-st-stutter even more."

"And if you're stuttering more, and if you're running for class president, how in the world will you be able to manage that?"

Caitin starts barking. She doesn't like hearing me and Dad argue.

"If I didn't r-r-r-r-r-r-run, Dad, you'd b-b-b-b-b-be happy because Mack and Suzy would be happy, and Suzy's m-m-m-m-m-mom would be happy. And since she's your g-g-g-g-girlfriend . . ."

"She's a friend, that's all."

"What did she s-s-s-s-s-s-s-s-say about our d-d-d-d-d-d-declaration?"

"We haven't discussed it. Jayson, can I tell you what I really feel?"

"You're g-g-g-g-g-going to tell me anyway, so g-g-g-g-g-go ahead."

"I feel like this campaign for president is putting too much pressure on you. Dr. Dan is right. Your speech seems to be getting worse. Rather than stop seeing him, I think you should start seeing him more. Rather than once a week, he's recommending that you see him twice."

"N-n-n-n-n-n-n-n-n-n-n-n-n-no."

"Will you at least think about it, son?"

I don't answer. At that moment, all I can feel is more anger. Anger at Dr. Dan. And now anger at my dad.

CHAPTER 17

Debating About Debating

The next morning, it's raining, but I slip out and walk to school anyway before Dad gets a chance to offer me a ride. I'm not ready to talk to him. Just as the bell rings for homeroom and I'm about to sit at my desk, Ms. Wolfson tells me to go to Principal Goodman's office. I'm nervous. It's never a good thing to be called to his office.

When I arrive, Mack is already there. He seems to know what's up.

Mr. Goodman is seated behind his desk. His curly black hair is a little off-center. It has to be a wig.

"As you both know, the position of class president and

vice president are almost never contested," he says. "Candidates are usually unchallenged. That's because the position itself is essentially honorary. That will change in high school, but here in middle school, we feel that students are still too young to establish a governing body with any real power. We think of it as practice. But because there are, in fact, two candidates, I have decided to give the students a chance to hear from you both. With that in mind, we will have a series of three debates between now and Election day. One next Tuesday, the second the following Thursday, and the final one on Monday before the election. Each debate will begin with an opening statement. Then I will ask questions, followed by your closing statements. Is this agreeable?"

My heart is racing. I knew I'd have to give at least one speech. But suddenly I'm hearing that I'd have to speak—and speak at length—three different times! Not only that, I'll be questioned by a man I don't like—and a man who doesn't like me. I have a feeling that Mack and Principal Goodman have discussed this plan beforehand. I feel trapped.

Struggling to get out the words, I say, "I'm n-n-n-n-n-n-n-n-not s-s-s-s-s-s-s-sure."

"What are you not sure about?" asks the principal.

"I d-d-d-d-d-d-d-don't kn-kn-kn-kn-kn-kn-kn-kn-know."

"Well, if you're going to run for office," says Mr. Goodman, "you're going to have to speak and speak clearly."

I take offense. I want to say to him, *You're using my stutter against me. You want to intimidate me so I'll decide not to run.*

Then, to my shock, the principal actually says the words. "If you don't want to run, Jayson, now is the time to say so."

Mack just sits there smugly, like he already has the election in the bag. He probably does.

It takes forever for me to get out the word: "N-n-n-n-n-n-n-n-n-n-no."

"No what?" asks Mr. Goodman. "No, you'd rather not run?"

I repeat the word: "N-n-n-n-n-n-n-n-n-n-no."

"Young man," says the principal, "if you are unable to make yourself clear to us, how do you expect to address the full student body?"

"Look, Jayson," says Mack, "if you'd rather not run, I can understand that. You can still hold your head high. You're an awesome athlete and student."

Mack and Goodman think they'll frighten me out of the race. I'm upset, so upset that speaking becomes even more difficult.

I stop and take a deep breath. Then I stand up. Standing up helps. I look first at the principal and then at Mack.

"I'm r-r-r-r-r-r-r-r-r-r-r-running."

"Well then," says Mr. Goodman. "We shall proceed. As a matter of fact, given your willingness, Jayson, I think it might help to add an additional debate. Let's not have three debates, let's have four. One per week."

"I like that idea," says Mack.

I hate that idea but feel too frustrated to protest. I've fallen into one of Mack Gaines's traps like a fish on a hook. It's too late to wriggle out.

I have basketball practice after school. Now I have to face Mack as a rival in the election and then try to be his teammate, and I don't have Chuck by my side. He usually helps me keep things in perspective. I have to work really hard to put the campaign aside before practice.

Coach puts us in a scrimmage game on opposite teams, and I end up fouling him three times.

"You trying to prove something, Linden?" Mack asks.

I don't respond. I'm afraid of what will come out of my mouth.

* * *

After practice, I meet Gloria at Rubato's to plan our campaign strategy.

"You l-l-l-look down, Jayson," she says. "What's wrong?"

I explain what happened in Principal Goodman's office and fill her in about the four debates.

"G-G-G-G-Goodman's buddies with the mayor," I say. "And the principal h-h-has it in for me."

"They're t-t-t-t-trying to scare you off," says Gloria, "but they didn't."

"I'm p-p-p-p-p-pretty scared. Four debates is a lot. Even one debate is a lot. I'd rather have n-n-n-no debates. You're the debater, not me."

"Did Goodman say anything about me debating S-S-Suzy?"

"No."

"That's b-b-b-b-because they don't think girls are important enough to d-d-d-debate."

"Or because they know you'd c-c-c-crush Suzy."

"This is actually good, Jayson."

"How is it g-g-g-g-good when I h-h-h-hate talking in public more than anything in the w-w-w-world? And now I'll have to t-t-talk four times. You should have seen me in the p-p-principal's office. I could hardly get out a single word."

"Yes, but you s-s-stood your g-g-g-ground."

"There were only t-t-t-two people in there, Principal Goodman and Mack. Imagine what my sp-sp-speech will be like when I'm facing the whole school in the auditorium. Even worse than that, G-G-G-G-Goodman has appointed himself the moderator. You know he's g-g-g-g-going to favor Mack."

"You're thinking about this the wrong way, Jayson. This is a break for us. This is our chance to start presenting our platform. We want to make our school a more inclusive place. You'll be able to s-s-s-s-surprise them. For each debate, you'll have a d-d-d-d-different issue."

"But if Goodman is running the debate, he might have t-t-t-t-topics of his own."

"You can switch subjects on him. You can take over and get our m-m-m-m-message out there. Tell everyone the changes we want to make when we are elected!"

"Not if I can't g-g-g-get the words out."

"I think you should s-s-s-start seeing Sylvia. She can help you."

"My dad told me that I should keep seeing Dr. Dan."

"And what did you tell your dad?"

"I s-s-s-said I was through with him."

"Great! And he's already given you permission to see Sylvia, right?"

"Yes, but he's n-n-not happy about it. Dr. Dan is his f-f-f-friend."

"But if y-y-you don't feel Dr. Dan is supporting you, that's all that m-m-matters."

"You might be right."

"I know I'm r-r-right. Come with me to my s-s-s-session with her tomorrow."

"It can't hurt."

"It can only help," says Gloria.

That night, I fall into another one of those scary I-can't-speak dreams.

This time I'm not standing on the stage of our school auditorium. I'm standing near mid-court in the Chase Center, where the Golden State Warriors play. The place is filled to capacity. Everyone is standing. Every eye is on me. A spotlight is shining on me. When I look to my left, I see Steph Curry and Jayson Tatum standing next to Dr. Dan. When I look to my right, I see Gloria standing next to Mrs. Best. I look around for my dad, but he isn't there. Chuck's not there either. Principal Goodman is dressed up as a clown. He wears a lopsided red wig and oversize floppy shoes. Before giving me the microphone, he whispers, "We have to reschedule your speech. A hurricane is heading in this direction. In ten minutes, it will destroy the Chase Center and everyone in it. Tell the people to evacuate. Tell them to get out now! It's all on you!"

Then he hands me the microphone.

Then I hear the wind howling.

Then I try to speak.

Then I try to say, *Get out! Get out now! Get out before it's too late!* but it's like my voice box is stuck.

Then Gloria says, "You can do it! We're all counting on you! You can save us!"

Then I try even harder. But the harder I try, the more I feel stuck. I keep trying to substitute different words, but nothing works. I can't say, *Get out!* I can't say, *Run!* I'm completely blocked.

Then the wind howls louder.

Then the roof blows off and the rain comes down, but no one is moving.

Then Dr. Dan comes up to me and takes the microphone out of my hand.

Then Dr. Dan says, "Jayson has a problem. He can't find fluency, but I can speak for him. The hurricane is almost here. Run!"

Then everyone starts to run. I run to look for my father, my friends, Caitin . . . but they're all gone. The hurricane is ripping the Chase Center apart. Chairs are flying. People screaming. People trampling other people. I fall to the floor, and when I look up, I see that Mack is trampling me.

I wake up in a cold sweat.

CHAPTER 18

Fear Is Real

A few days later, I explain the dream to Sylvia in our first solo session.

"I love that dream," she says.

"I'm glad someone d-d-d-does," I say. "It s-s-scared me to death. It seemed so r-r-r-real. Wh-wh-what's to love about it?"

"Because you were able to express all your fears," Sylvia says. "All your fears were packed inside that one dream. But you tell me, Jayson. What do you think the dream says is your biggest fear of all?"

"I'm afraid when it comes time to t-t-t-talk in public, I

won't be able to get out a single w-w-w-word."

"Has that ever happened?"

"I haven't s-s-spoken very much in public. Actually, I d-d-d-d-don't think I've ever spoken in public besides when teachers call on me in class."

"But when you speak in school, or even when you speak to a waiter in a restaurant, you're speaking in public, aren't you?"

"I guess so."

"And have you ever not been able to get a word out?"

"I've st-st-stuttered a lot."

"But ultimately you say what needs to be said. Isn't that right?"

"I guess so," I say.

"Yet the fear is real," says Sylvia. "How does it make you feel about the campaign?"

"I am afraid," I admit. "I'm afraid of all these d-d-d-debates. I'm afraid I won't be able to g-g-g-get out a word. Or even if do get out some w-w-w-w-words, I'll make a fool of myself."

"Do you think stuttering makes you sound foolish?" asks Sylvia.

"I know it always m-m-m-m-makes me feel bad."

"I'm going to give you a little assignment. I want you to think about situations where you feel bad or frightened about speaking. Really try to imagine those feelings and stay with them, rather than trying to avoid them or push them away."

I think about debating the rest of the night—as I'm finishing my homework and feeding Caitin and lying in my room. Then I text Gloria about my appointment.

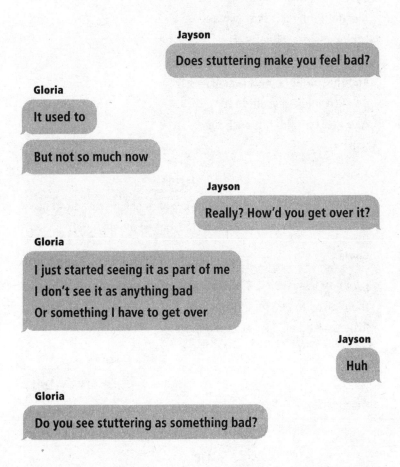

Jayson
Does stuttering make you feel bad?

Gloria
It used to

But not so much now

Jayson
Really? How'd you get over it?

Gloria
I just started seeing it as part of me
I don't see it as anything bad
Or something I have to get over

Jayson
Huh

Gloria
Do you see stuttering as something bad?

Jayson

I don't see it as something great
I get tired of how it makes me feel
I get tired of feeling ashamed

Gloria

Yeah. I know that feeling
I've definitely felt that way
I think it's pretty natural
But there are things that I like to do,
and they require me to speak
So I just made myself do it
And I was afraid. But each time,
a little less so

Jayson

So you're never scared to talk
in front of people now?

Gloria

I wouldn't say never. But a lot less
than I used to be. Sometimes I get a
little worked up, like at that debate

Jayson

Haha I was too!

110

Gloria

And that's not great for stuttering either. But we feel what we feel. At least that's what Sylvia says

Jayson

Yeah, I guess she has a point. But what about the campaign?

Gloria

What about it?

Jayson

What if my feelings make me mess it up? The first debate is coming up so soon. What if I'm not ready?

Gloria

Why are you sure that's going to happen? You're already campaigning, right? People are paying attention. People liked the declaration. I'd say your feelings have gotten you pretty far

Jayson

I guess that's true

CHAPTER 19

Back to Kindergarten

The week before our first debate, Sylvia has given me another "assignment." I'm starting to have doubts about this switch. Who knew that a new therapist would mean extra homework? I have even more doubts when Sylvia wants to take me to a kindergarten class taught by her husband, Ted. I ask her to explain the purpose.

"Sometimes Ted has older kids come in to read to his five-year-olds," she says. "They love it. I think you'll love it too. Besides, in its own way, it'll help prepare you for your first debate."

"How?"

"You'll see."

As it turns out, Ted teaches at Stephen Foster Elementary, the very same school I used to go to. The weird soapy smell of the classroom gives me a funny feeling in my stomach. I don't have great memories of the place because that's where my stutter first began. It happened, just like it happened this year—on my first day at school when the teacher asked me to say my name. After I explain that to Dr. Fine, she says, "I understand, Jayson. But I see it as something you can work through. Another negative you can turn positive."

I get permission from Dad to go with Sylvia to her husband's class. Ted is a friendly guy with long hair that practically touches his shoulders. He's wearing a Jayson Tatum Boston Celtics number 0 sweatshirt and Levi's jeans.

When his wife introduces me, he catches me checking out his sweatshirt.

"I grew up in New England," he says with a smile. "I love the Celtics."

"I like Jayson Tatum," I say, "but for me, it's Golden State all the way."

Jokingly, he says, "I'm sure we'll learn to get along anyway. The kids are excited that you're here. I've picked out a book I think they'll like."

There are fifteen kids in Ted's class, and I have their

complete attention. If they were adults or even kids my age, it might be intimidating. But I like how they look up to me, like I'm someone special. He's chosen *The Little Engine That Could*, which was a favorite of mine when I was their age.

Usually reading out loud is the last thing in the world I want to do. It's when I stutter the most. But reading to five-year-old kids is different. I'm not at all scared. Besides, I love little kids. I've always wanted a little brother or sister.

"You can sit on a chair," Ted says, "or if you're more comfortable, you can sit on the floor."

I sit on the floor. I want to be close to the kids.

"This is a b-b-b-b-book my daddy read to me when I was your age," I say.

"What's it about?" asks one of the girls.

"It's about t-t-t-t-trying really hard and g-g-g-g-getting where you need to go," I say.

"You have b-b-b-b-b-bumpy speech," says a freckle-faced boy. "I have bumpy s-s-s-s-speech too."

I haven't heard that expression before. I like it.

"Yes," I say, smiling. "I have b-b-b-b-bumpy speech."

The kids gather around me. I read slowly and, before I start each page, I show them the illustration. I feel relaxed. I love the expression on their faces. Their mouths are slightly open and their eyes wide. Even when I hit a "bump," not a single kid turns away or looks uncomfortable or tries to guess what I'm about to say next. They just listen. The story is about a train carrying toys and food for kids. But to deliver those toys and food, the train has to go over a mountain, and it needs the help of a little bright blue engine who comes along at just the right time. Huffing and puffing, the little blue engine keeps saying that, yes, he can do the job. And in the end, he does it. He delivers the toys and food.

The kids love the happy ending and begin clapping their hands. The boy with the bumpy speech even shouts, "Hooray! The engine d-d-d-did it!"

Ted thanks me for reading the book. I thank him. A couple of the kids want to give me hugs. Hugs all around. It feels great.

Sylvia drives me back to Bloom Middle School. On the way, she asks, "Well, what do you think?"

"It was great!"

"How do you feel about your speech?"

"Well, I st-st-st-st-stuttered much less than usual."

"Why do you think that is?"

"I was less n-n-nervous than usual."

"What made you less nervous, Jayson?"

"Little kids are just little kids. I don't feel like they're judging me."

"And when you speak in front of kids your own age, what happens?"

"If they're my f-f-f-friends, not much."

"And if they're strangers?"

"I st-st-st-stutter," I say.

"And feel bad about it?"

"Well, it's the first impression they g-g-get of me."

"And you see it as a bad impression."

"I g-g-g-guess so."

"But with these little kids today. . . ."

"I didn't care."

"That's interesting. You didn't care?"

"Or, I just didn't th-th-think about it as much. I was f-f-f-focused on the story and enjoying their r-r-r-reaction to it."

"You were okay with them seeing you just the way you are."

"I g-g-guess so."

Sylvia nods and smiles.

CHAPTER 20

Big Barbecue at the Mayor's House

Mack has invited the entire basketball team to his home for a party on Friday night. He's also invited the cheerleaders. I don't really want to go, but as a member of the team, I don't see how I can avoid it.

As Chuck and I are playing some one-on-one the day before, he convinces me I should go.

"M-m-m-maybe I c-can pretend to be sick," I say.

"C'mon, Jayson," he says. "You're our man on the inside. You have to tell us about how it's done at the mayor's mansion. Are there gold toilets? The biggest TV screen in the world? People who make sure your soda doesn't have too many bubbles?"

"All right, all right," I say.

"Make sure you find out the dimensions of that TV."

On Friday, I arrive at the mayor's house the same time as some of my teammates. We high-five each other and head into the house. The first thing we see is a fancy winding staircase. Overhead is a gigantic chandelier. The floor is made of marble, the walls covered with huge paintings of horses and dolphins. It's a lot to take in. It really is a mansion. A maid leads us through a huge sunken living room, a dining room the size of a bowling alley, and, finally, into the den, where the party has started.

"Just in time, guys," Mack greets us with a big smile.

Thinking of Chuck, I have to laugh a little because on the wall behind him *is* the biggest flat-screen TV I've ever seen. The game's about to begin.

The Golden State Warriors are playing the Nets in Brooklyn. After Jayson Tatum, Kevin Durant is my second-favorite non-Warrior. I always want Golden State to win, but I love watching K.D.

"Jayson! Over here!" Mack calls. He gestures to a seat near him and Suzy.

Suzy gives me a big smile that, weirdly, almost doesn't seem fake. Mack hands me a bowl of popcorn.

I don't know how to react, so I just go along with it. I'm excited about watching the Warriors-Nets game, especially on a screen big enough to be in a movie theater.

The game goes great. Golden State jumps off to a commanding twenty-point lead and never looks back. Steph Curry can't be stopped. That puts everyone in a great mood because the score's not close. Still the Nets are always dangerous on defense.

Mack whistles. "That looks like the play you made the other day, Jayson."

"Wh-wh-what? G-g-get real!"

"Seriously, though, your defensive game has improved a lot. Your shooting too."

"Thanks." I'll never get used to Mack being nice to me. Then, suddenly, Suzy chimes in.

"Your dad seems really nice," she says.

"H-h-he's all right," I say. We laugh uncomfortably. I guess I should say Suzy's mom seems nice too, but I'm just not feeling it. I just want to change subjects. Luckily, Curry scores again before too long, and I get a reprieve. Mack high-fives me. The Nets are totally crushed. The game is over practically before it begins.

* * *

After, we start talking about Curry's field goal percentage and his three-pointer technique. We guess at how long it must have taken him to just be able to make those shots from anywhere, and how no one will ever match his three-point record. Mack sees I know as much about Curry's stats as—maybe even more than—he does. When it comes to basketball, we both have a lot to say. And because we both root for the same team, there's no disagreement. Why can't Mack always be this nice at school and to my friends?

After the game, everyone goes outside, where Mayor Gaines, Mack's dad, grills steaks and hot dogs on their porch. Beyond the grill is a big pool, and beyond the pool is a huge basketball court. Even before we have time to digest our food, my teammates and I choose sides and hoop for thirty minutes or so. Mack and I are on the same team. Shockingly, he passes to me and lets me shoot—unlike during our scrimmages at practice. He pats me on the back when I score. Near the end, I can't help myself. I have to take one three-pointer. I'm sure I'll miss, but to my surprise, it goes in.

"Nothin' but net, Linden. You must be channeling your inner Curry!"

"I guess so! M-m-maybe we all have one."

When we get back inside the house, Mack's mom serves us chocolate cake and ice cream.

I'm eating my cake when Mack says, "Well, the debate is almost here. Are you ready?"

"I think s-s-s-so."

"I'm looking forward to it," he says before changing the tone of his voice. "As long as you don't pull any funny stuff."

"What do you m-m-m-mean by f-f-f-f-funny stuff?"

"I don't know, Jayson. You and Gloria can be pretty tricky. Have any new declarations to make?"

"That wasn't a t-t-t-trick," I say. "We w-w-w-were just s-s-s-s-saying what n-needed to be s-s-s-s-said. S-s-s-some changes n-n-n-need to be made."

"All the kids at school like the school the way it is."

"Not all the k-k-k-k-kids."

"Most of the kids."

"We'll s-s-s-see," I say.

Mack glares at me. "Did you see how our Warriors wiped out the Nets today?" he says icily. "Well, that's what I plan on doing to you at the debate."

I don't even respond. I get up, thank his parents for having the party, tell my teammates goodbye, and leave.

* * *

"What was it l-l-l-l-like?" Gloria asks when she calls later that evening.

"Weird."

"W-w-weird how?"

"His house is amazing. His p-p-p-parents seem cool. He has this humongous TV."

"Of course," Gloria says. "You're b-b-best friends now?"

"Nah. You kn-kn-kn-know better. Watching the game was fun, the food was great, he was super nice, except at the end when he said he'll crush me during the debates."

"He w-w-w-w-was just trying to get in your head, Jayson. Just trying to c-c-c-c-c-confuse you."

"Well, I'm confused enough without M-M-M-Mack going into his Dr. Jekyll–and–Mr. Hyde routine."

"I know, Jayson. It's confusing that Principal Goodman w-w-wouldn't let us suggest a topic for each debate."

"What did he say? 'The element of surprise will make the debates more interesting.' That doesn't make any sense. It's just a way for him to control e-e-e-e-e-e-everything."

"Sure, he's a control f-f-f-freak," says Gloria. "But that doesn't mean you can't bring up the issues we want to raise and bring to everyone's attention. And I think our d-d-d-decision for you to s-s-s-start off with gender-neutral bathrooms is right. That will g-g-get everyone's attention."

"I'll do my best," I say. "B-b-b-but it's only th-th-th-three d-d-days away." Just the thought of it is making my stutter worse.

"You'll do great, Jayson."

"I h-h-h-hope so."

CHAPTER 21

Crunch Time

I wake up Tuesday morning super early. Dad knows it's debate day and asks me if I'd like something special for breakfast. I'm not really hungry, but he's nice enough to make my favorite, buttermilk pancakes. I can't even eat a whole pancake. I'm too nervous.

On the way to school, Dad says, "I'm sure you'll do great, Jayson."

"Thanks, Dad," I say, wishing I could be as sure as he is.

I have three classes to get through before lunch. I see Chuck in English, and we talk afterward. He doesn't ask me about the debate, but he does ask me about the mayor's house.

"Was it swanky?"

"Wh-wh-wh-what do you think?" I say.

"Heh-heh. And that TV?"

"B-b-b-big," I say.

"Man, I asked for exact dimensions," he says.

"N-n-next time. But know, you could probably see it from space."

"Oh, that's how it is?"

"Yeah, right."

"Well, how was Mack?"

"W-w-w-w-well, he w-w-w-was nice . . . until he w-w-w-wasn't."

"That sounds about right." Chuck laughs. I tell him about the home theater Mack has and the basketball court. I don't realize until it's time to go to lunch that for a little while I have forgotten all about the debate. Chuck knew I needed to talk about other things to get my mind off it. He's good like that. Finally, the bell rings, ending the third class. I'm off to lunch with the Bloom Squad.

Halfway through lunch, though, the debate is all I can think about. It's the period afterward. I keep looking at my watch and wiping my hands on my pants. All my friends are encouraging me. And random students keep coming up to me to say positive things. I'm basically saying nothing. I'm trying to save all my energy for the debate. I'm rehearsing some ideas in my head, but since I'm not sure what the topics are, I can't really prepare that much.

We walk over to the auditorium. Attendance is voluntary, since it's during study period. The setup is simple. Three chairs onstage. Mack on the right. Principal in the middle. Me on the left. A sea of chairs for the students in the audience. My heart's beating like crazy. I've never been this nervous before. I breathe in for four counts and out for four counts. Then in for five and out for five. I focus on the poster at the far end of the auditorium from when the Bloom Bobcats won the county basketball championship. I try to imagine nothing but kindergarten students in the audience. I think I can, I think I can. . . . There's no stopping the fear, though. Sylvia's right about that. Instead of trying to push it away like I normally would, I try to sit with it. It's not easy, though.

Principal Goodman taps the mic. "Let's start by introducing yourselves and giving your credentials. By that, I mean all your extracurricular activities. Mack, would you mind starting off?"

Mack smiles at him and begins to speak. "Most of you know me. I'm captain of the basketball team, captain of the debate squad, and an honor-roll student. It would be a privilege and an honor to become class president. And I'd do everything in my power to represent the Bloom Bobcats in the best way possible."

At first, the auditorium is only half full. But while Mack is speaking, I see dozens of students filing in. When Mack is done, everyone gives him a standing ovation, even though he hasn't really said anything. When the clapping dies down, the attention turns to me.

"Jayson, please introduce yourself and do the same," Principal Goodman says.

I see my friends seated in the front row. They raise their fists in unity. I feel a burst of energy.

"I'm Jayson Linden, and I have something I'd like to propose."

I say all that without stuttering! I'm amazed and happy. I'm sure I can get through the whole thing without stuttering.

"Before any proposal, Jayson, please follow the form and give your extracurricular credentials," Principal Goodman says.

I shake my head. "That's not what's important. Everyone

knows I play basketball, and I'm proud to be on the honor roll. But it's more important that I represent those who have had trouble being heard. There are students who have been trying to present a proposal for gender-neutral bathrooms and more inclusive policies to avoid discrimination."

I'm on a roll. *I'm fluent! I'm speaking fluently!*

Principal Goodman butts in. "What does that have to do with the election of a class president?"

"As far as I'm concerned? Everything," I answer.

Principal Goodman frowns. "Those aren't things we want to discuss right now."

"I don't know who you mean by 'we,' but I'm me and I want to discuss it."

"You can't. This forum is not designed to—"

"I th-th-th-thought this was a debate. Aren't d-d-d-d-debates about d-d-disagreements?" I ask.

I start to stutter. My frustration is building up.

"This first debate is about qualifications," says Goodman. "Why do you think you're more qualified than Mack?"

"B-b-b-b-b-b-b-b-b-b-b-because I have ideas on how to solve i-i-i-i-i-issues and make our school more inclusive."

"But this isn't anything we've discussed beforehand. It's as though you're launching a surprise attack," Principal Goodman says.

"W-w-w-w-well, you sh-sh-sh-should know s-s-s-s-something about that. . . . Y-y-y-you . . ."

I know what I want to say. I want to point out that Principal Goodman has already surprised me on more than one occasion. That he refused to let us choose topics in advance. That *he's* the one who launches surprise attacks and I just want to lay out the issues in our campaign, but suddenly I'm too frustrated to get it out the way it is in my head.

"Wooo!" shouts Gloria as she stands up. "Yeah, Jayson!"

"You got this, Jayson," Chuck says.

"We're counting on you!" says Amia.

I know they're being supportive. I try to focus on them and not my stutter.

"Now let's get back to the subject at hand," Principal Goodman says.

"B-b-b-b-b-b-b-b-b-but you haven't even l-l-l-l-l-l-l-l-l-l-let m-m-m-m-m-m-m-me . . ."

And then the nightmare comes true. I can't say the word "say." I can't get it out. I can't say, *But you haven't even let me say anything about my proposal.* I can't get past the word *me.*

And neither Mack nor Principal Goodman bail me out. They just sit there as I struggle to say a word I can't get out. I think of the tools that Dr. Dan has given me. Go soft on the consonant and stress the vowel. I try to say *sAAy*, but that doesn't work. I try to compose myself and breathe. Breathe in, breathe out. Now try to say "say." But that doesn't work either. Start again.

"L-l-l-l-l-l-l-l-l-let me s-s-s-s-s-s-s-s-s . . ."

I still can't say "say."

There's a ripple of laughter that starts small and gets stronger until eventually it's all I can hear. I'm sure everyone in the auditorium is laughing. But then my friends shout, "Stop laughing!" but that only makes the laughers laugh louder.

Finally, Principal Goodman stands up and says, "Let's stop this first debate right here. I think we can agree that we're not going to get much further today. I need to rethink this format. Everyone, please leave the auditorium in an orderly fashion. You are all dismissed."

CHAPTER 22

Tuesday Tacos at Tortilla Flats

After the debate, I don't want to talk to anyone, not even my friends. I've blown it. I've messed up. I hate myself. I hate my decision to run for class president. I should have known better. I'm angry at myself, angry at Mack, angry at Principal Goodman, angry at the world. I don't say a word in the rest of my classes, and I just want to go home and hide.

When I get home, Dad is in his study. I don't want to tell him what's happened. I go straight to my room and turn on an episode of one of my favorite TV shows, *Young Justice*. I wish I was in that show. I wish I was a superhero cartoon character living a cartoon life. I don't like the life I'm living.

I don't like being a person who stutters. I hate stuttering. I'm so embarrassed. How am I going to be able to face my classmates again?

Dad can tell something's wrong. He can probably guess the debate didn't go well, and he's nice enough not to ask me anything about it. Instead, he reminds me that it's Tuesday and Tuesday always means tacos at Tortilla Flats. Tortilla Flats is the best Mexican restaurant in Bloom. We've been going there forever, and their beef tacos are my favorite.

Since I was too nervous to eat my breakfast or lunch, I'm starving. But it'll probably take more than tacos to take my mind off everything.

During the ten-minute car drive, Dad and I stay silent. The restaurant is crowded, but luckily we get the last open table in the back. I look around to see if any of my classmates are there. I spot Marge, a girl from my algebra class, and Tony from social studies. They both wave at me. I'm sure they were at the debate. They saw me at my worst. My cheeks flush red.

I study the menu like I'm seeing it for the first time.

"You mean you're not ordering beef tacos?" asks Dad.

"Maybe I'll try something else today."

"I'd be surprised, but get whatever you want."

When the waiter comes around, I stick with my favorite

and order beef tacos. Dad smiles.

While we're waiting for the food, the silence goes on so long someone has to say something. Dad breaks the ice.

"I heard you had a tough day, son," he says.

"Who'd you hear it f-f-from?"

He hesitates.

"Suzy's m-m-m-mom?"

Dad realizes he's made a mistake. Now all he can do is nod.

"What did Mrs. Best say?" I ask.

"Only that it wasn't easy for you."

I feel like crying. I feel like shouting. I don't want to discuss what happened. So, I don't say anything.

The waiter arrives with our food, so luckily I don't have to answer. I devour my meat tacos, and they're delicious but they don't make me feel better.

"Want to go to Sweet Stuff for dessert?" asks Dad when we're finished eating.

Sweet Stuff has homemade ice cream.

"No, I'm good," I say.

On the drive home, Dad brings up the subject again.

"I know you don't want to discuss it with me, and that's fine. I understand. But I am wondering whether Dan—"

"I already told you, Dad. Dr. Dan is no help."

"Then how can I help? How can anyone help, Jayson?"

"I like Sylvia."

"Dr. Fine?"

"Yes."

"It's fine with me if you want to continue seeing her."

"I d-d-do," I say.

When we get home, I climb into bed to finish the rest of my homework. There's the low rumble of thunder in the distance, and Caitin settles in beside me, the way she always does before a big storm. Big raindrops batter the windows. The storm sounds angry, just like me.

CHAPTER 23

It's Out of Your Hands

I set up a session with Sylvia for the next day after practice. Being on the court with Mack just makes everything worse. I can't believe I have to be on a team with him. I'm looking forward to getting to Sylvia's office. I need to talk to someone who really understands me. I need to talk to her.

But when she lets me into her office, I don't say anything. Instead, I sit down and burst into tears. She sits next to me and hands me a tissue. I take a few deep breaths to try to stop crying, and dab at my eyes. She returns to her chair.

"Crying can feel good," she says. "It can be a release. And

a relief. I know it's hard for boys to cry. It can feel humiliating, can't it?"

I nod.

"I'm glad you feel you can trust me, Jayson. Feelings are just feelings. They come and go. But one thing we can do is look at them. We can talk about them. We can try and understand them. But what we don't want to do is judge them."

"I don't want to feel ashamed of crying, and I don't w-w-w-want to feel ashamed about stuttering, but I do."

"And it's great to hear that. Because I know you're telling the truth. Your truth."

"I don't know what happened. I was really fluent at the start. I didn't stutter at all. But then I s-s-s-s-stuttered so much, the principal had to stop the whole debate."

"I'm sorry to hear that. But things change. Life is all about change."

"But how is this ever g-g-g-going to change? There are m-m-m-more debates coming up. And what am I supposed to d-d-d-d-do? I thought you had a plan, Sylvia. I thought the plan was to get me to read to the kindergarten kids to prepare me to speak in the d-d-d-debate. But it didn't p-p-p-p-p-prepare me. It didn't prepare me at all."

"The idea wasn't to prepare you, Jayson. The idea was

just to give you a different kind of experience in speaking before people."

"I was fine with little kids. But in front of kids my own age, I f-f-f-fell apart."

Dr. Fine pauses for a moment. "Let's talk about what happened yesterday at school. You said you were excited at the beginning when you weren't stuttering at all, right?"

"Right."

"You felt great because you were presenting yourself as a fluent speaker."

"I was doing g-g-g-great."

"So not stuttering is always great. And stuttering is always *not* great."

"Something like that."

"But what if I told you there's a good chance you'll be stuttering for a very long while. Maybe forever. Do you hate hearing that?"

"I don't love it."

"But can you accept that it's possible?"

"I know it's p-p-possible," I say.

"And if I tell you that you can lead a perfectly wonderful life as a person who stutters, does that seem possible?"

"I guess it's p-p-p-possible."

"So what if we forget the idea of eliminating your stutter?

What if we throw that idea out the window? Would you be willing to think about that?"

"I don't know."

"Listen. There is a benefit to accepting your stutter. By not focusing on that, you eliminate the worry about whether you're going to stutter or not. You are going to stutter. In fact, the next time you speak in front of the school . . ."

"You really think there's going to be a n-n-n-next time?"

"Of course I do," says Dr. Fine. "You wouldn't be here if you weren't determined to see this thing through. But next time will be different."

"How can you be s-s-s-s-sure?" I ask.

"Because you can make it different. You can stutter on purpose. You can stutter on the first word you say."

"Why w-w-w-would I do that?"

"To announce yourself as a person who stutters. You see, when you started out yesterday and spoke with fluency, you were thinking—and tell me if I'm wrong—that maybe stuttering was all behind you. Maybe the miracle had happened. Maybe the entire school could see you as a perfectly fluent speaker and you wouldn't stutter once. But the truth is that you're a different kind of speaker. And if you make that clear from the beginning, you're being honest and open and accepting yourself just the way you are."

I keep listening. It sounds crazy at first, but something about Sylvia's argument is starting to make sense to me.

"In other words," she goes on, "you stand up and you stutter and say, 'I, Jayson, am a person who stutters.' And in saying that, you end the war."

"What war?" I ask.

"The war inside you when one side says, 'I'm not going to stutter, I'm not going to stutter,' and the other side says, 'Yes, you are, yes, you are.' You let the stuttering side win. And when it wins, when you not only know you're going to stutter, but when you make yourself stutter on purpose, you may be able to relax. You may be able to finally say, 'I'm a person who stutters. That's who I am. And even if sometimes I hate that, sometimes I can accept that. Sometimes I can live with that. And sometimes I don't even care.'"

"And that will make me s-s-s-stutter less?"

"I'm not saying that, Jayson. It may make you stutter more. But I believe with all my heart that it will help you avoid what happened yesterday. It will prevent you from breaking down and help you keep going. I'm thinking that you stopped yesterday because the war being waged inside your head was too much to take. It would be great to try to put an end to that struggle."

"And you think I can do that?"

"I know you can."

"I'll try h-h-h-harder."

"I know you're determined, Jayson, and I admire that about you. But maybe the idea isn't to try harder. Maybe the idea is to try less. Don't push so hard to be fluent. And try more to present yourself the way you are."

"And if I feel b-b-b-bad about the way I am?"

"That's a perfectly legitimate feeling. But it's a feeling that will pass. And I believe, with self-acceptance, it's a feeling that will change. Every day we change in countless ways. You felt one way when you walked in here today, and I'm guessing you're feeling another way right now."

"I am."

"So, there you go. Feelings are always in motion. Imagine feelings like a basketball on the court. It rolls off fingers, to the hoop, off the rim, into another set of hands. The coach may have a plan; the players may have a plan. But the ball doesn't. It's just being moved from one end of the court to the other. Sometimes it may move according to those plans, but sometimes another force is involved—it doesn't hit the floor quite the way it's expected to, there's another player in the way. Sure, it moves according to the laws of physics, but humans can't always manipulate physics in the way they want to. There are too many unknown factors. That's kind of like your stutter. You can make a plan. You can take certain measures to improve fluency, but in the end, it's a force of its own and so are your feelings about it."

"I didn't know you like b-b-basketball, Sylvia."

"I'm guessing Steph Curry is your favorite Warrior, Jayson. Mine is Draymond Green. I like the way he's always passing the ball."

"Draymond knows the game."

"He's cool under pressure."

"I want to be cool under pressure," I say.

"You already are, Jayson."

By Friday, the week of nonstop thunderstorms has passed, and the sun is beaming in. Caitin licks my face good morning. After my session with Dr. Fine, I'm feeling stronger.

On our drive to school, Dad can tell my mood has improved.

"Talking to Sylvia helped, huh?" he says.

"She's cool."

He doesn't ask me to describe my session. He knows I don't like talking about what goes on in therapy. Instead, we talk about my first basketball game of the season.

"I l-l-look forward to it, but then I picture us on the court without Chuck, and it takes s-s-some of the fun out of it."

"I know, buddy. You two have been playing together a long time."

"There's got to be a way to get him b-b-back on the team."

When Dad drops me off and I walk into school, a lot of kids snicker when I pass them in the hallway. I guess that's to be expected. But my friends are waiting for me by my locker. As they rally around me and give me a group hug, suddenly those snickers from the other students don't seem so important.

Gloria says, "Th-th-th-the thing you were afraid of h-h-h-h-happened. And look, you're still here. Still ready to go."

"And you'll only be stronger next time," Chuck says.

"Everyone has bad days," says Preeda.

"It had to be rough for you, Jayson," Amia says, "but you had the guts to speak in public, and you put the issues out there. I think people admire that."

"Thanks," I say.

"You're going to speak again, aren't you?" Amia asks.

"I g-g-g-g-guess so."

"You have to, Jayson. You have to show them."

"Show them wh-wh-wh-what, Amia?"

"Just show that you're not scared," they say, "even if you are."

I laugh. That makes sense.

"We have a surprise for you," says Chuck.

Gino reaches under the table and pulls out a couple of posters. They say, *Vote Linden and Lopez. Linden* is in green and *Lopez* is in yellow.

"The school colors," I say.

"Exactly. We want you guys to represent the whole school," Amia says. "So, you're up for it, aren't you?"

I hear something in their voice that makes me say, "I won't quit. I p-p-p-promise."

Amia gives me another hug.

I love my friends. And I'm going to try hard not to let them down.

CHAPTER 24

Mack's Offer

On Monday, just as I feel like my courage is building back up, I get a note to report to the principal's office.

Oh no. Here we go again.

When I arrive, Mack is already there. He's actually in the middle of a conversation with Mr. Goodman. That makes me uneasy.

"Oh, here he is now," says the principal. "Mack and I were just talking about you."

That makes me even more uneasy.

"Mack was just saying that . . . well, given your challenges when it comes to public speaking, there might be a better way to even the playing field."

"What d-d-d-does that mean?" I ask.

"No more debates," says Mack. "Look, Jayson, I don't want to put you through this whole thing again."

"You d-d-d-didn't put me through anything," I say.

"Well, you know what I mean," says Mack.

"No, I don't," I say, even though I do.

"What I'm saying, Jayson, is that you and I can forget the debates and the speeches and do it all on paper."

"I think Mack has a sound idea," Principal Goodman chimes in. "And I congratulate him for having such a sporting attitude about it. You can express your views about whatever subjects you like in the school paper. We've already discussed it with Sam Hall, the editor."

Sam, aka one of Mack's best friends.

"No one d-d-discussed it with me," I say.

"That's what we're doing now," says Mr. Goodman.

"It doesn't feel like a d-d-d-discussion," I say. "It feels like you've both already made up your minds."

"Only for your sake," says Mack.

"Th-th-thanks, but I'll stick with the debates," I blurt out. Principal Goodman and Mack both look surprised. I've even surprised myself.

"Why?" asks the principal.

"Why not?" I ask back.

"To save you the embarrassment."

"M-m-m-m-maybe I don't m-m-m-mind being embarrassed. H-h-how about you?"

"Look, Linden, we just want to save you the humiliation," says Mack.

That last remark is meant to be insulting. I remember what Gloria said about Mack trying to get in my head. So even though I'm mad, I take a deep breath and stand up. "See you at the next debate," I say on my way out.

CHAPTER 25

Vote Linden and Lopez!

After school, I go to Rock 'N Bowl, where Chuck, Gloria, Amia, Preeda, and Gino are using one of the empty alleys to make more *Linden and Lopez* campaign materials. They're turning it into a party. There's paint, paste, markers, stickers, glitter, all being put on poster board. They're also making buttons and banners. Everyone's into it.

I don't want to be a party pooper, but I feel like I have to tell my friends about the meeting with Principal Goodman and Mack. When they hear the story, they get mad.

"It was another Mack trap," says Chuck. "They want to shut you up."

"They want to get you to doubt yourself," says Amia.

"N-n-no kidding. It al-almost worked too," I say.

"But it didn't?" asks Gino.

"Nope. I just smiled and th-th-th-thanked them for their 'concern.'"

"Ha-ha-ha! That's how you do it!" Chuck says. We fist-bump.

"Th-th-th-they want to shut us up!" says Gloria as she stands. "They won't let me d-d-d-debate Suzy. Now they want to cancel your d-d-debate with Mack. But it's not going to work, right?"

"Right!" we all say together.

"W-w-we'll s-s-stand up and speak for as long as it takes to get our m-m-message across," says Gloria. "We're not afraid!"

"All right!" says Amia.

"Maybe that should be your s-s-s-slogan," Gino says.

"What do you m-m-m-mean?" I ask.

"'Vote Linden and Lopez! We are not afraid!'"

I think about that for a second.

"Well," I say, "except we are sort of a-a-a-afraid, aren't we?"

"Everybody's afraid sometimes," says Chuck, "but not everyone takes on their fears. You're both more *not* afraid than you are afraid. 'We are not afraid!' works. Let's go with it."

Everyone says yes, including me.

Since I first started talking about running for president, I had relied on my friends to lift me up—and it worked for the most part. But usually once I was home alone, I would start to stress about the campaign. I'd be doing the dishes or my homework and out of nowhere I'd think about Mack's big phony smile, or Goodman pinching his caterpillar eyebrows together, and I'd get mad. Then I would feel down about the whole thing and decide that maybe I should just give up.

But it was different today. The mantra is running around in my head as we're making the posters and then as I'm walking home. I'm still thinking about it as I put my key in the door and set my stuff down on our kitchen table. Even after I've done my chores and my homework, it's still there. That night, when I'm playing with Caitin out in the backyard, watching her run after the tennis ball over and over again, I keep thinking, *We are not afraid! We are not afraid!*

I *am* not afraid.

CHAPTER 26

On Again, Off Again

The school day goes by on Tuesday without any word about the official time for the next debate. I don't know how to plan for it, or if I should be writing my arguments out on paper. It was bad enough worrying about the debate I knew was going to happen, but at least then I could prepare.

Then just before the last bell of the day rings, I am called to the principal's office. You would think it would be no big deal by now, but you'd be wrong. My heart is in my throat. I try to remember the mantra, the slogan: "We are not afraid." Which really means we are not afraid of our fear. When we feel it, we face it.

We are not afraid. We are not afraid. I say it to myself as I put my books in my backpack and shrug it onto my shoulder. Of course, by the time I collect all my stuff and get to Mr. Goodman's office, Mack is already sitting in front of his desk.

"I've decided to let the debates continue," Goodman says. His hair is pushed to the opposite side today, and his eyebrows are smushed together seriously. They are so distracting I almost miss what he's just said, but Mack's response drives it home.

"Awesome!"

I don't say anything. I'm happy that I'll get to talk about issues that I believe in, but I'm also scared about repeating what happened the first time. *We are not afraid*, I remind myself.

"When will the next debate happen?" asks Mack.

"Friday," says Principal Goodman.

Friday is awfully soon. It's the day after our biggest game of the season against our toughest rival, Blair. Maybe I'll spend so much time thinking about the game I won't have that much time to worry about the debate. I just hope it's not the other way around.

"Does that work for you?" asks Mack.

"Sure," I say.

That night, Gloria comes over and helps me prepare the points I want to make sure to hit in the debate. We go over all the things I want to talk about and work into the conversation. As always, she's encouraging.

"Y-y-y-you're doing great, Jayson," she says. "R-r-r-remember, you're s-s-speaking as a person who s-s-s-stutters. And you have people on your side. I think we've started to w-w-w-w-win over a lot of the other kids."

CHAPTER 27

Bobcats vs. Bears

O ur gym is filled to capacity—cheerleaders are doing somersaults, the crowd is cheering, and we're all warming up. Lots of people come out for the big game of the season—students, parents, teachers, little kids, aunts and uncles. We're playing against the Blair Bears. Blair is the next town over from Bloom, and the Bears are our biggest rivals. Last year, they won state. Their average player is about three inches taller and weighs about fifteen pounds more than our average player. I'm not sure what they feed them over there, but I'm thinking I should make a campaign promise to smuggle some of it into Bloom. The north side of the gym is filled with white and gold—their colors.

Our side is slightly fuller since it's a home game. People are holding up green-and-yellow *GO, BOBCATS* signs, and some have signs for individual players—there are a few for Mack. I have my own little cheering section—Chuck, Gino, Amia, Preeda, and Gloria are all there. Gloria's holding up a sign with #23—my number—on it. I wave. It's nice to see them up there, but I'd still rather have Chuck in the game with me than in the stands. I don't see my dad yet, but that's not too surprising. It takes him a while to leave the office sometimes, but he'll make it before the tip-off. I'm sure of it.

Even with all the time I've spent on my campaign and speech therapy, I've never missed a practice with the team, and I'm gradually getting better at keeping the campaign from interfering with the teammate dynamic I have to maintain with Mack. My midrange jump shot is improving along with my rebounding and general defense. But I know I'm not good enough to start yet. I don't play a minute during the first half, and we're down by ten. It's tough to be on the sidelines when we're behind. Coach Croft usually gives everyone a little playing time, but not tonight. Tonight, he's more concerned about winning than worrying about substitutes. I look up shortly before halftime to see Dad sitting next to Mrs. Best. They both wave at me. I wave back. He's been out with her a few more times since the night of the disastrous dinner. I try not to think about it too much. I just really want to get in the game and play.

Finally, with four minutes left and us trailing by only six, I'm substituted for the first-string power forward, who has twisted his ankle. Mack is playing point guard. After number 17 on the Bears misses a corner three, I grab the rebound and pass it to Mack. He takes it downcourt all the way for an easy layup.

"Good pass, Linden," he shouts out loud enough for everyone to hear. On defense, I'm able to grab a second rebound. This time I take the ball down the court myself. When I see that Mack is heading toward the hoop, I throw up a lob that he catches and throws down for another two points. Now we're only down by two.

Amazingly, I get my third consecutive rebound, and before I can pass the ball to Mack, I'm fouled. If I hit both shots, we'll be tied. I stand behind the foul stripe and take a deep breath. I hear Dad yelling, "You can do it, Jayson!" I release the ball and watch it bounce off the front of the rim. One miss, one to go. I take another deep breath. I've been practicing free throws for years. I'm a good free-throw shooter. I know it's all about relaxation. No one's guarding you. No one's between you and the hoop. I can do it. Except

I can't. My second free throw rattles in the basket and then rattles out. Cheers from the Bears side. I feel awful.

Coach takes me out of the game. From the bench, I watch the Bears extend their lead back to six. And then Mack goes on a run. With a minute left to play, he hits two threes in a row to tie the game. On the other end of the court, they call a foul against us, and number 14 on the Bears hits one of two free throws, putting them a point ahead. The clock shows ten seconds to go. Mack dribbles the ball downcourt and is fouled in the act of shooting. That means if he's able to do the very opposite of what I had done and hit both shots, we'll win.

He stands at the foul line. On both sides of the gym, everyone is standing. Everyone is nervous, everyone cheering.

Mack's first shot is nothing but net. He's tied the game.

His second shot is almost a duplicate of mine: the ball rattles around the rim, but instead of bouncing out, it goes through.

We're up by a point.

A Bear grabs the rebound but, in passing the ball, throws it out of bounds. We bring the ball in and pass it around just to run out the clock. Mack has won the game for the Bloom Bobcats.

"Mack! . . . Mack! . . . Mack! . . . Mack! . . . Mack! . . .

Mack! . . . Mack! . . . Mack!"

I'm cheering too, but instead of calling Mack's name like everyone else, I'm saying, "Bobcats . . . Bobcats." I can hear a section of audience start to join me, and when I look up, I see Gloria, Chuck, Preeda, Amia, and Gino in the stands. I wave to them. There's no denying that Mack led us to victory, but it was a team effort.

Later that night when Dad, Caitin, and I are sitting on the couch watching TV, he says, "Jayson, your passing looked sharp tonight. But I'm guessing you have mixed feelings about the win."

"Everyone likes w-w-winning," I say.

"Well, you're a good sport, Jayson."

"Thanks, Dad."

"Competition brings out the best in us."

"That's what they s-s-s-say."

"Good night."

"Good night, Dad."

The game was great and the excitement lasts for a while, but once it goes away, I lie in bed thinking of how in the world I'm ever going to win the debate tomorrow. I want to. I want to win big. I remember my conversation with Sylvia. I think about what wanting this means, and how it will make me feel to lose. I remember the last debate and how hard it was. Then I decide that wanting it just means I want to do my best and use my voice. Maybe that's not just about fluency but presenting my case and the issues I want to talk about. I want it not just for me, but for my friends and fellow students. I take a big breath and hold it; then I let it out slowly.

I look down and see Caitin, cuddled up in her dog bed, looking up at me. The great thing about Caitin is that she doesn't know about winning basketball games or debates. All she knows is that she loves me.

CHAPTER 28

A Person Who Stutters

I wake feeling rested. Even though it took me a while to fall asleep, I didn't have any nightmares. I'm pretty calm during my first three classes. I'm calm at lunch with my friends. After lunch, we all go to the auditorium for the debate. This time, there's not one empty seat. I wonder who's waiting for me to do what I did last time—get stuck on a word and blow the whole thing. I know there are people out there rooting against me, but I focus on my friends, who are all giving me a thumbs-up. That really helps.

Mack and I sit on opposite sides of the stage again, with

Principal Goodman in the middle. I have won the coin toss, so I go first. I look over the auditorium at everyone. Some people are looking at me, some are looking down at their phones. Principal Goodman asks us what qualifies us to be president. I say my first words in front of the crowded auditorium.

"I am a person who s-s-s-s-stutters."

I stutter on the word "stutters" on purpose, taking Sylvia's advice. Rather than try to hide my stutter, I announce it. I can't say that I'm proud to stutter, but I can say that I'm proud to make the announcement that I do stutter.

I glance over at Mack standing at the second podium next to me. He seems confused. Good. The more confused he is, the happier I am.

"Jayson," says the principal, "please tell us about your qualifications for class president."

"You asked about that last t-t-t-time. This time, I just wanted to start off by s-s-s-saying that I stutter and sometimes it might take me a while to g-g-g-get out a word."

There are a couple of *WHOOP*s from the corner, and I don't have to look to know where they're coming from. A couple of kids in the back also cheer. But mostly, there's silence. In saying it, though, I feel a lot better. It always feels good to tell the truth.

"My qualifications are that I'm on the high ho-ho-ho-ho-honor roll, I'm in the advanced-placement English c-c-c-class, also the advanced-p-p-p-p-placement social studies class, and I'm on the basketball t-t-t-team. B-b-b-but maybe my s-s-stutter qu-qu-qualifies m-m-m-me most of all. It's what m-m-makes me unique."

Another big cheer comes from my squad in the corner. Mr. Goodman turns to Mack for his turn, and he lists the same qualifications from last time again.

"Fine," says Mr. Goodman. "Now I'll ask each of you this question: What would be your first act as class president? Mack, you're up first."

"Ask the school to redo our gym. Compared to other schools, it doesn't measure up. Blair's gym is twice the size of ours."

"Jayson," says the principal, "how do you feel about that?"

"I th-th-th-think g-g-g-gender-neutral bathrooms are a b-b-bigger priority."

"To put in gender-neutral bathrooms," says Mack, "we'd have to take all the urinals out of the boys' room. That's a waste of money. That money could be better used to fix up the gym."

"The gym is fine the w-w-w-w-way it is. Gender-neutral

bathrooms will help a lot of kids who are f-f-f-figuring out their identity."

My friends in the auditorium start cheering, and a few more people join in.

"I'm not sure the school board would take up that issue," says Mr. Goodman.

"They might," I say, "if we p-p-p-p-p-present to them as a united school. If the st-t-t-t-t-tudent body elects a p-p-president who runs on that p-p-p-p-platform."

"The bathrooms don't need to be changed," says Mack. "Everyone's happy. No one's complaining."

"I'm c-c-c-c-complaining," I say. "And a-as p-p-president, I would s-s-speak up for th-th-those who don't feel comfortable s-speaking up."

"Bloom isn't a school of complainers," says Mack. "Bloom is a really happy school. We should be focusing on the good stuff."

Mack gets big applause mixed with boos from my friends.

"It's all about being positive," says Mack. "Positive attitudes lead to happiness. Wouldn't you agree with that, Jayson?"

Mack has found a way to turn the tables against me. Anger grips my chest and I feel myself tightening up. I worry that my speech will mess up again like it messed up last time. I have no doubt that Mack wants that to happen. How should I answer the question: Do positive attitudes lead to happiness?

I take a deep breath and, rather than go into a long explanation, simply say, "N-n-n-n-n-n-not always."

"When is it bad to be positive?" asks Mack.

"For example," I say, "if you're having different feelings about your gender identity, and you go to a school that doesn't r-r-r-respect those feelings, you're going to feel bad. You're going to f-f-f-f-f-feel disrespected. You're going to have to p-pretend you're s-s-s-something you're not. You c-c-c-can't make yourself feel positive when your school doesn't c-c-c-care about your feelings."

"You're making up an issue that no one really cares about," Mack says.

Another big round of applause for Mack. But boos and shouts from my supporters, who seem to be growing in size.

"I-it's easy to think that n-n-no one cares about it i-i-if you focus on wh-what makes y-y-you h-h-happy and ignore everyone else. M-m-maybe that's w-w-worked f-f-for you so far, Mack."

"OH!" Chuck shouts from the corner.

Principal Goodman breaks in and says, "Now hold on a second, Jayson. I'm afraid we might be a bit out of our element here. This is a question of funding. We lack the funding for new bathrooms. The new president and the student council have no say-so about funding."

"Why n-n-n-not?" I ask.

"Because," he says, "that's the way it is. It's the way it's always been."

"Well, it sh-sh-sh-should change."

Gloria and the rest of the squad cheer loudly. Gloria has a big smile on her face. Preeda is pumping her fist. Amia is waving their arms back and forth. Chuck is whistling and clapping his hands. And lots of other students start joining in!

"Students are students," says Mr. Goodman, "and administrators are administrators. Students can't decide school funding."

"P-P-P-P-P-P-Principal Goodman," I say, "with all due respect, shouldn't this debate be between m-m-m-me and Mack? It feels like I'm d-d-d-debating you."

The silence is deafening. Principal Goodman's caterpillars are clenched into an angry tuft above his narrowed eyes. There is no noise in the auditorium with the exception of a few chair squeaks and coughs. Finally, Principal Goodman replies.

"You make a good point, Jayson. And since we both feel

this is counterproductive, let's put an end to it, shall we? This debate is over. You're all dismissed. Collect your things and report back to class."

There is so much chatter it's like a roar. No one seems happy about what just happened.

"W-w-we need to find a way to finish this debate the r-r-r-right way. How do you feel about that, Mack?" I ask.

"I'm willing to debate you anywhere, anytime about any subject."

"G-g-g-g-great," I say. "Maybe the best thing is just to have you and m-m-m-m-me talking without anyone in between."

"Fine with me," says Mack.

Everyone around us—all my friends, all Mack's friends—agree.

In the hallways after the debate, I'm feeling better. Kids other than just my close friends come over to pat me on the back and say I've done a great job. After my first debate performance, a lot of kids didn't think I'd show up again.

"You showed up," says Chuck, "and really got under Goodman's skin. He was sweating. He had no clue what to say."

Just then, Principal Goodman's voice comes over the loudspeaker. Everyone in the hallway stops to listen.

"Listen up, students. After careful consideration, I've decided that the current campaign for class president will continue without any further debates. Any events resembling a debate held off school grounds are not to be considered as part of the race for class president. This decision is final."

A chorus of boos—from practically everyone, including Mack and his friends.

"Can he do this?" asks Chuck.

"He just did," answers Amia.

Mack and Suzy walk over to us. "I don't like it," says Mack.

"Me either," I agree.

"I think we need to keep debating. Otherwise, it's not a fair election. We both had more to say," says Mack.

"I think so t-t-too."

"You have any ideas of how to do it?" Mack asks. "We'll just have to do it outside school."

"How about Rock 'N Bowl?" says Chuck. "I can get Dad to close it down for an hour after school. It's big enough for practically everyone. You guys can debate there."

"Why don't Suzy and I d-d-d-debate as well?" asks

Gloria. "Shouldn't the students hear from their future vice president?"

"Are you good with that, Suzy?" asks Mack.

"If Gloria's in, I am," says Suzy.

"I j-j-just hope you're ready," says Gloria.

CHAPTER 29

Girls First

The next Friday, tons of students show up at Rock 'N Bowl. Everyone likes the idea of defying Principal Goodman by having a debate.

Beforehand, Suzy, Mack, Gloria, and I get together and decide this debate will be between Suzy and Gloria. Ours will come a week later, just before the election.

Chuck's dad sets up microphones in front of Big Al's restaurant, where Suzy and Gloria, sitting on stools, face the kids. Some students are standing, some sitting in chairs, some on the floor. I'm sitting right in front of Gloria, who starts it off.

"I'm g-g-g-g-glad we've decided to have no moderator. I'm glad we've decided to handle this ourselves. I'm also glad that Suzy agreed to this. Principal Goodman wouldn't even allow two g-g-g-g-girls to debate."

At the sound of the words "Principal Goodman," the crowd boos.

"With all that in mind," says Gloria, "I'd l-l-l-like Suzy to start and say whatever is on her mind. How she feels about the chance to become c-c-c-c-class vice president."

"Thank you, Gloria," says Suzy. "I'm also glad we have this chance. I think it's great to talk about what we'd do as class officers. I'd want more dances. Many more dances. Right now, all we have is the end-of-school spring dance. Shouldn't there be a school dance before the Christmas holiday? And how about a school New Year's party? We could even start a cookie or bake sale and use the proceeds to hire a professional DJ, rather than just using a playlist. I also want to say that it wouldn't matter if you have a date or not to go to these dances and parties. These wouldn't be events for the elites. They would be fun for everyone. Everyone needs a break from schoolwork. Come to the dances with a group of friends. Or just come alone. Don't worry about having a date. Just come to have a good time and know you're part of the Bloom Middle School community."

Suzy's speech gets heavy applause from the crowd.

"Go, Suzy!" shouts one of her friends.

"Now it's your turn, Gloria," says Suzy. "Are you against dances?"

"No," says Gloria. "I love d-d-d-dances. And I love to dance. I think what you're saying is fine. B-b-b-but I also th-th-think s-s-s-students deserve to be heard. P-Principal G-G-Goodman and the s-s-s-staff m-m-make decisions all the t-t-time that affect us and our s-s-s-school. Th-th-they ch-ch-change th-th-the size of s-s-s-sports teams on a whim. Th-th-they k-k-keep p-p-people from d-d-debating b-b-based on s-s-s-speech limitations. Th-th-they decide what issues can be b-b-brought to the school board. You would th-th-think it was th-their school. But who's s-s-school is it?"

"Our school," a few of us shout in response.

"WHOSE SCHOOL?" Gloria asks. She holds her hand behind one ear.

"OUR SCHOOL!" comes the reply, louder this time.

"WHOSE SCHOOL?" Gloria demands again.

"OUR SCHOOL!!!" This time nearly the whole group is yelling in unison.

"That's right. That's why I'm p-p-p-proposing that, as your p-p-president and VP, J-J-J-Jayson and I act as your t-t-true representatives. W-w-w-we will approach the s-s-school board with proposed ch-ch-ch-changes. That way these d-d-decisions aren't being made behind our b-b-backs anymore."

A big whoop goes up from the corner. Then Amia shouts, "Whose school?"

"OUR SCHOOL!!!"

Big Al comes out of the kitchen grinning and nodding. The debate pretty much ends there, with Gloria and Suzy laying out their feelings. Everyone is too fired up to pay much attention anymore. I hear someone say, "I can't believe they wouldn't let that girl debate. She's awesome."

It is hard to tell which way the votes are going to go, but I couldn't be prouder to be Gloria's running mate and friend.

CHAPTER 30

H-O-R-S-E

That Sunday afternoon, Chuck and I are playing H-O-R-S-E at the playground by my house for nearly an hour, and he's crushing me. After my fourth loss in a row, I'm ready to stop, so we take a break. We sit on the grass and look up at a sky filled with puffy clouds. It's chilly, and it feels like rain. The wind is blowing, but the fresh wind feels good.

"You played a good game last week against Blair," says Chuck.

"I did all right," I say.

"Look, you were only in for four minutes; I'd say two assists and three rebounds isn't so bad."

"Those f-f-free-throws, though."

"Yeah, okay. I see what you mean."

"Ha! Th-th-thanks a lot."

"Heh. You know I'm joking. Now if I had been out there . . ."

"I w-w-wish you had been. I'm s-s-s-s-still mad about that."

"I'm not," says Chuck. "It doesn't really matter. Mack's always going to be the star of that team. He's always going to control the team. The coach is always going to do what Mack wants. He's a great player. No Mack, no chance of a Bobcat championship."

"B-b-b-but maybe it d-d-d-doesn't have to be that way. You heard wh-wh-wh-what Gloria was p-p-proposing. M-m-m-maybe w-w-we can ch-ch-change things."

"Maybe. But honestly, I don't get my hopes up anymore. And anyway, we're more than teammates, Jayson. We're brothers. And when you win the election, the school will finally see that Mack is no superhero."

"It's going to take a superhero to b-b-b-b-b-beat him. And I'm no superhero."

"Superheroes are make-believe. They're fun to watch. But they're not real. A lot of the kids are really liking the way you've brought up these issues. They know it takes guts to do what you've done," Chuck says.

"I haven't d-d-done anything yet."

"You've driven Principal Goodman nuts. I say that's doing a lot."

My phone buzzes with a text from Gloria.

Check this out, she says.

She's sent a link to a TikTok video of Gloria and Suzy's debate posted from Preeda's account. There are fifteen hundred views—nearly twice the number of Bloom Middle School students.

CHAPTER 31

Summit Meeting

D ad and I are eating dinner—fresh vegetables and brown rice he's cooked up in the wok—when he surprises me by saying that Principal Goodman called him earlier in the day to request a summit meeting the next day.

"What does that m-m-m-m-mean?" I ask my dad.

"I'm not sure, Jayson. All he said was that we need to come in and talk about the campaign. He says it's gotten out of hand."

"Did he say who's going to be there?"

"You, me, Mack and his parents, Gloria and her parents, Suzy and Laura, and, of course, Principal Goodman."

"Did h-h-h-he say what it's about exactly?"

"I asked, but he wouldn't go into specifics."

"Sounds like he f-f-f-found the video."

"What video?"

I get my phone and show him.

"Wow. That's a pretty fiery speech," he says.

"It really was. P-p-people were into it. I think th-th-they're tired of just talking about d-d-decorating the g-g-gym for the spring dance."

"That's exciting, Jayson!"

"Even if w-w-we get in t-t-trouble?"

"I don't see what rules you've broken. The debate wasn't held at school."

"Th-th-that's true. Y-y-you n-n-never know with Principal Goodman."

Later in my room, I check out the video again. It's up to five thousand views. I don't see how that can be possible.

"Oh boy, Caitin. This is going to be interesting."

The way Caitin looks at me makes me think that she understands what I'm saying.

"I'm kind of scared of what Mr. Goodman has up his sleeve," I tell Caitin. "I don't really trust him."

Caitin perks her ears. I can feel her agreeing with me.

"He definitely has something against me."

Caitin barks.

"He's really a strange guy."

Caitin growls.

"You don't think he's going to kick me out of school, do you?"

Caitin turns her head as if to say, *Can he really do that?*

"That man," I tell Caitin, "might do anything."

The next morning, I ride my bike to school. As I'm locking it up, Gloria appears beside me.

"Hey, you," she says.

"Goodman saw Preeda's TikTok?" I say.

"I was g-g-g-guessing the s-s-s-same thing," she says.

I'm fidgety and nervous during my first two classes. The last person in the world I want to see is Principal Goodman.

I'm dismissed from my third class to go to the meeting. I'm surprised that it's not in Principal Goodman's office. It's in the big conference room.

On one side of the table are me, Dad, Gloria, and her folks; on the other side are Mack and Mayor Gaines, and Suzy and Mrs. Best. Principal Goodman sits at the head.

"I'm sorry Mrs. Gaines couldn't be here, Mr. Mayor," says the principal.

"She's visiting her sister in London," says Mr. Gaines.

"Now," says Mr. Goodman, "let's begin. I thank you all for coming. I know your time is valuable, and therefore I'll be brief. I gave strict orders that there be no further debates for the campaign for class president and vice president, and yet those orders were disobeyed. Both Gloria and Suzy participated in a debate at the local bowling alley. Apparently, my authority held no weight. Therefore, I'm asking you, the parents, to join me in enforcing the ban."

"I don't understand the reason for the ban," says Mr. Lopez.

"Things were getting out of hand. Candidates are bringing up issues that are beyond the authority of the student council."

"Why can't we b-b-b-b-bring up any issues we want?" asks Gloria.

"Issues like gender-neutral bathrooms should have nothing to do with a student election," says the principal. "That's not a student decision."

"I agree," says the mayor.

"I don't," Mrs. Lopez says. "They're student bathrooms, and the students use them. Students should have a forum to discuss them. In the same way there should be some transparency in how advisers make decisions. My daughter was not able to have the position she wanted on the debate team because of her speech."

"I don't know anything about that," says Principal Goodman.

"That's interesting," says Mrs. Lopez. "Perhaps you should."

"There is video, though," says the principal, "of your daughter leading some kind of a chant. A protest against me and my staff members."

"That was just p-p-p-part of the d-d-debate," Gloria says. "J-J-J-Jayson and I are asking f-f-f-for students t-t-to have m-m-m-more of a voice."

"A debate I banned," Principal Goodman said. His wobbly cheeks turn red, and the caterpillars practically jump off his face in excitement.

"I don't know how you can ban something that's not on school property," says Gloria's dad.

"Mr. Lopez," says Mr. Goodman, "I must remind you that this is merely a middle school. Issues like renovating bathrooms are the business of the school board."

"Your principal makes a good point," the mayor says to his son.

"But that's not the p-p-point," I say. "How c-c-c-can he ban something that's not at school?"

"I agree with Jayson," Mack adds. "We have something to say and should be able to say it. Principal Goodman can ban us from debating at school, and that's fine. We didn't disobey that ban. Suzy and Gloria debated at a separate location, and it went great. There was no trouble. If Jayson and I want to debate, why not? We give you our word that we will not use the school grounds for any debate. Isn't that true, Jayson?"

"Yes," I say. Mack is really surprising me. I'd never guessed he'd go against his father.

"And Gloria and Suzy?" says Mack.

"I agree," says Gloria.

Suzy nods.

"So that's it," says Mack.

"Son," says the mayor, "I think you're missing your principal's point. You're raising issues that aren't your concern."

"Th-th-they are our concern," I say.

"Mayor Gaines," says my dad, "no one has broken any rules here."

"But, Ian," says Suzy's mom, addressing my father, "these children have started bringing attention to public issues they're not capable of really understanding."

"But these decisions affect them," Mrs. Lopez says quite firmly. "The more empowered they feel, the better their community will be. If they feel that the school doesn't care what they think, then why should they care either? These issues—gender-neutral bathrooms, discrimination about who can and cannot debate—are important to everyone. We should be grateful that they care enough to speak up."

Squirming in his chair, Principal Goodman huffs a few times. He's not happy.

He says, "I brought you here to enlist your aid. I hear and respect everyone's opinion, but I need to be able to count on your support if things get out of hand. Can I?"

"You certainly can," says the mayor.

"Of course," echoes Mrs. Best.

"If things get out of hand, yes," says Mr. Lopez. "But I haven't seen that happen yet."

"I trust my son," Dad says. "I know he will do what he thinks is right."

As we leave, I see that the mayor is annoyed with Mack, though Mack doesn't seem to care.

He and I give each other a quick nod. We see things the same way, almost like we do on the court.

CHAPTER 32

Chronicles of Bloom Middle School

The next morning during announcements, Principal Goodman calls off the election.

"In the past few weeks, the eighth-grade class campaign has become a distraction to students and their studies. As much as we like to provide students with extracurricular opportunities to practice leadership, classes and discipline must come first. It is for that reason . . ."

I don't even listen to the rest. It's hard to hear it over all the noise anyway. I guess maybe you'd expect I would be upset, but it is clear right away that Principal Goodman has made a huge miscalculation. Everyone is upset. Nobody can focus for the rest of class—or any of the classes leading up to lunchtime. And of course, the discussion only gets more intense in the cafeteria. Everyone is outraged at this decision. The funny thing is all the usual cliquey tables are all mixed up. Everyone's talking to everyone because we're all in it together.

"Boy, he really had to dig for that one," Amia says. "We're 'too distracted'?"

"M-m-m-maybe we should show him how distracted w-w-we can get," I say.

"Ha! Linden's right," Mack says.

By the end of lunch, almost everyone has signed on. Instead of going to our afternoon classes, we all go to the hallway. We chant "OUR SCHOOL" and post our protest to TikTok. Principal Goodman doesn't know what hit him. He announces something over the intercom, but no one can hear it. The bell rings, dismissing everyone.

When Dad picks me up later, he asks, "Anything interesting happen at school today?"

I look at him. He starts to laugh. I know right away he's gotten a call from the principal.

"Well, I said I trusted you to do the right thing. I guess you figured out what that was."

MIDDLE SCHOOLERS MAKING THEIR MARK

by Ford Hanson
special reporter for the California News

Things are not what they used to be at the Bloom Middle School. Elections for eighth-grade class president and vice president, usually uneventful yearly rituals, have turned into high drama. It all began when the candidates for president—Mack Gaines, son of Mayor Gregory Gaines, and Jayson Linden, son of local architect Ian Linden, faced one another for two debates in the school auditorium.

Things quickly got out of hand—so much so that R. Dewey Goodman, principal of the school for the last 35 years, called off the debates.

"They were promoting ill will and serving no real purpose," the principal remarked.

Despite the ban, debates continued and even expanded. The two girls running for vice president—Suzy Best and Gloria Lopez—invited students to their debate at Rock 'N Bowl, a local bowling alley.

"I can't say whether it was because we're girls or because we're running for vice president," Gloria Lopez commented, "but we were never given a chance to express our views at school. So, we decided to express those views in a setting outside school."

"Students need to be heard. There are issues like the need for gender-neutral bathrooms, and better rules for extracurricular activities that affect all of us," commented Jayson Linden. "The debates offered us a chance to make our voices heard. That's why Principal Goodman canceled them."

It seems that the young candidate may have a point. After a clip of the debates became a local viral sensation, Goodman canceled the election. The students responded by organizing a protest during school hours.

"Bloom Middle School has always had elections," said Mack Gaines, "and it's never been a distraction. Principal Goodman just doesn't want us to have a real debate."

Principal Goodman's office responded by

saying that the principal has always welcomed student voices and he's not about to stop now. His only concern was that campaigning was a distraction from education.

"We will resume the race for eighth-grade class president and vice president effective immediately. As debates have never been a part of the race in the past, we will not be holding any debates in the future."

The students say they plan to hold one final debate at the local theater.

CHAPTER 33

Wildflower Lake

The Saturday before the big Tuesday debate. Gloria and I are walking the nature trail around Wildflower Lake, the prettiest spot in Bloom. The November air is chilly. People pass by, but no one we know. Gloria is wearing a black hoodie that her folks had custom-made for her. In bright white letters, her sweatshirt reads, *We Are Not Afraid!* I wear a regular Bloom Bobcats sweatshirt and a Golden State Warriors cap. I'm not feeling great. Mack and I have agreed on a final debate. I thought it would be easier this time, but it's not. Even worse, the debate is being held at the local theater's auditorium. The whole thing has attracted so much local media attention, you would think it was the race for the presidency of the United States.

"You'll f-f-f-feel better," says Gloria. "It's just nerves."

"It's m-m-m-more than nerves," I say. "I can't help feeling Mack is manipulating the whole thing. I feel like he's manipulating m-m-m-me."

"Why do you s-s-s-say that?"

"He's gone against his d-d-d-dad. He's gone against Principal Goodman. He acts like he's on our s-s-s-side about having these debates. But he also knows that making them so public is s-s-s-scaring me. I think he's hoping I'll ch-ch-ch-choke like the first time."

"Let him hope whatever he w-w-wants to hope, Jayson. But we know better. We know you're g-g-g-going to do great."

"B-b-but it's gonna be all over th-th-the internet and on local TV. T-t-t-talking in f-f-f-front of a bunch of k-k-kids my own age was bad enough."

"I'd b-b-b-be scared too, Jayson," says Gloria.

"You're saying that to make me f-f-feel better. You're not afraid of anything."

"I'm scared of lots of things, J-J-J-Jayson. I'm scared that you'll be too scared to g-g-go through with this whole thing. I'm scared M-M-Mack will get his way by using all this f-f-fear against us."

We stop walking and sit on a bench overlooking the lake. A mother duck is leading her ducklings across the water. A flock of birds fly overhead. The sky is overcast with a thick blanket of dark clouds.

I turn away and look at the words on Gloria's hoodie.

"You always liked our s-s-s-slogan," I say. "Now you're saying it isn't true."

"Sure it's t-t-t-true, Jayson. But nothing's true all the time. Sometimes I get scared. If I pretended that I wasn't a little s-s-scared for you, I'd be lying."

"Let me ask you something, Gloria. What would you s-s-s-say if I told M-M-M-Mack to call off the whole thing? Would you be m-m-m-mad at me? Wouldn't everyone be mad at me?"

"I think everyone would understand. Like you said, everyone s-s-s-sees that Mack's running the show. Everyone would just say, 'Jayson's tired of Mack running the show.' You have an out if you want one."

"I've been t-t-t-trying to think about what he's g-g-g-going to talk about, and I have no idea."

"Well, at least you know what you and I and all the others have been t-t-t-talking about. You have our ideas all planned out."

"But what if his ideas are better than ours?" I ask.

"What if it starts r-r-r-raining right now and we don't even have any raincoats?"

"We'll get w-w-w-wet."

At that moment, it does start to rain. We both laugh. The harder it rains, the more we laugh. Even though we get soaking wet, we don't care. The rain feels good.

The rain comes back to me that night in a dream. Only this time, there's loud thunder and lightning bolts. There are tornadoes lifting up our home, the glass box, and smashing it to bits. Where is Dad? He's crushed under the house. I try to get to him, but the rain turns to hail, and the hail turns into razor blades slicing up my arms. I have to stop the dream. I force myself awake. I look at the clock. Two a.m. I can't fall back to sleep. Caitin wakes up the same time I do. She looks up at me to see what's wrong. I can't lie to Caitin. I can't lie to myself. I'm scared of Tuesday, more scared than of anything in my entire life. I go to my desk and look over all the notes that me and my friends have written for the debate. They don't seem as good as when we originally wrote them down. They seem weak. I feel weak. I feel like I want to get out of the whole thing. I know I need help.

CHAPTER 34

The Volunteer Fire Force

On Sunday, I ask Dad if it's okay if I see Sylvia for a special session. He agrees. When I call Sylvia, she invites me to her house, except it isn't a house. It's an old fire station that has been converted into a home. The lettering outside still says, *Volunteer Fire Force, built 1947.* Inside, the downstairs is one big room with couches and chairs and a kitchen at the far end. Ted is at the kitchen table playing Scrabble with their son, Warren. He introduces me to Warren, who goes to college in Berkeley. Sylvia leads me upstairs, where they've constructed two separate rooms. We go to Warren's old bedroom, which they've turned into a study. I'm glad to see a Golden State Warriors banner on the wall. Sylvia sits in a wooden rocking chair. I lean back into a beanbag.

"Beanbags aren't comfortable for everyone," she says. "You can have this rocking chair if you want, Jayson."

"I like bean b-b-b-beanbags."

"Tell me what's going on."

"You already kn-kn-kn-know."

"I read the article in the paper, if that's what you mean. But is there something I should know that I don't?"

"I'm not s-s-s-s-sure I can do it."

"I can understand that."

"Shouldn't you be telling m-m-m-me, 'Of course you can do it. It's a snap, Jayson.'"

"It isn't a snap. I imagine it's a struggle. A big struggle."

"I d-d-d-d-d-don't want the struggle. I'm tired of the struggle."

"Just like you're tired of your stutter."

"Yes! Exactly! I'm tired of s-s-struggling. Tired of having to p-p-p-p-prove myself."

"Who says you have to?"

"Everyone."

"Who's everyone?"

"Everyone is everyone. Everyone is the w-w-world."

"You must feel like the world's going to be watching you on Tuesday."

"That's exactly how I f-f-feel."

"You also must feel excited," Sylvia says.

"I am."

"I say that because you've worked so hard to get to this point."

"I d-d-d-don't see it that way."

"How *do* you see it, Jayson?"

"Th-th-that I'm about to fall into one of Mack's traps."

"Why?

I shrug.

"Through your persistence and courage, you've built a strong platform. When your campaign started, you mostly just thought about your stutter. But now it's grown bigger than that, hasn't it?"

"I g-g-guess so."

"I know so."

"But that's y-y-y-you telling the story, Sylvia. I can't tell the story that way."

"Why not? You have a choice of how to tell it. If you tell like you're the victim, you'll feel like the victim. But if you tell like you're still in control, you'll be in control."

"N-n-n-n-not of my speech. I s-s-s-s-still can't control my s-s-s-stutter."

"But that doesn't mean your stutter has to control you."

For so long, I've thought I couldn't control my stutter. In many ways, that was true. But now this woman is saying something else. She's saying my stutter does not have to control me. She's saying that I have a choice. I can tell one story that makes me feel bad: the story that says I'm trapped. Or I can tell another story that can make me feel good: the story that says I'm not trapped at all. I'm where I want to be.

Thinking about a packed auditorium, with stage lights and TV cameras pointed at me, how can I *not* freak out? I keep thinking back to the first debate with Mack, which had to be stopped because I couldn't get out another word. And that was only in front of our student body. Yes, I did better in the second debate, but that's because I had messed up the first debate so bad. The second debate was held in the same auditorium with the same kids. This third debate is so much bigger. Everyone's paying attention now.

Later that day, I'm at Gloria's house where, together with Chuck, we go over all the points I'll have to make Tuesday. We've reviewed them a dozen times before, but I want to review them another dozen times. Or two dozen times. Gloria and Chuck keep saying I'm completely prepared and have nothing to worry about. I keep saying that I feel unprepared and have everything to worry about. That night I barely sleep.

When I get to school Monday, everyone in the halls is buzzing. Everyone's excited about what's going to happen tomorrow. *Vote Linden and Lopez! We Are Not Afraid!* posters are pasted on the walls. There are even more posters that say, *Bobcat Pride! Vote Mack and Suzy!*

Everyone is taking up sides. And every side is saying they're going to win. My friends think we're gaining supporters, but Mack and Suzy's friends are saying there's no way we can win. We're still underdogs. A lot of kids come up and say encouraging things to me, but a lot of Mack supporters give me dirty looks. Even the teachers are talking about it. The air is thick with tension. My stomach is churning.

Then at lunch I'm called to the principal's office. I'm thinking, *Not again!* I take a last bite of my tuna fish sandwich, get up, and reluctantly make my way down the hallway.

When I arrive, Mack is already sitting there and Principal Goodman is scowling. "I realize that there is nothing I can do about the event that you have planned for tomorrow without my authorization. Your debate will be off-site and out of school jurisdiction. I've come to accept that as a reality. But in thinking about it, I've concluded that you both might benefit if I were the moderator."

It's clear that Principal Goodman just wants to be on TV.

"I don't think that will be necessary," says Mack. "Jayson and I can handle it by ourselves."

"I agree," I say.

The principal grunts. He's been foiled again.

CHAPTER 35

The Last Debate

The big day is finally here, and the local theater is packed. I knew there would be a lot of people, but I guess I wasn't prepared for what that would look like. Every seat is taken, and people are standing shoulder to shoulder in the back. A TV director shouts orders to camerapeople positioned on either side of the room in front, their lenses pointed toward the stage. Bright lights shine in my face.

I'm all the clichés: My stomach is in a knot, my palms are sweaty, my nerves are raw. I'm trying to act cool, but inside I'm not cool at all. I wonder if it shows. I'm sure it does show. Everyone knows I'm about to freak out.

But then I talk myself down. I do some breathing exercises. I think about Amia, Preeda, Gloria, Gino, and Chuck, who are sitting in the front row and wave when I look over at them. I try to focus on the changes we want to make. It soothes me for a minute, but then I start to worry about disappointing them. Back and forth, back and forth, my mood swings. One second, I'm confident. The next, I'm about to crawl under my chair.

Mack and I have agreed to flip a coin. The winner decides who goes first. I say heads. It comes up heads. I say, "Mack, you b-b-b-begin."

Sitting in matching straight-back wooden chairs in the middle of a bare stage, facing the cameras, Mack and I have finally come to the moment of truth. This is do or die. My first thought is that I've made a mistake. Having won the coin toss, I should have gone first and gotten it over with. Now I have to sit here, listen to him talk, and worry that I can never match his presentation. I look over again at my friends and their parents in the front row. Dad is sitting next to Gloria. Across the aisle, Mrs. Best sits next to Mayor Gaines and Mack's mom. If Principal Goodman is there, I don't see him. I do see Dr. Fine and her husband. Sitting next to them I see Dr. Dan. That surprises me and makes me happy. Dr. Dan smiles and waves at me. I think, *It's great that he's here. It's great that he and the Fines are sitting together. It's great to have their support.*

Wearing his green-and-yellow Bloom Bobcat jacket, Mack walks to the podium. As he arranges his notes on the lectern, I'm convinced that the outfit I've picked out—a plain blue blazer, a white button-down shirt, and khakis—is wrong. I should have worn something more colorful or something that had more school spirit. But it's too late. All I can do now is listen to Mack.

As he starts speaking, he's completely relaxed. It was as though he's been talking to massive crowds and television audiences his whole life. No hesitancy. No fear. He's a natural.

"I want to thank you for coming out and spending some time with me and my friend Jayson. I want to thank those in the audience and those watching at home. This is a great occasion for all of you to hear how middle school students think and feel. Before I begin, I'd also like to say that Jayson and I flipped a coin to see who'd speak first. He won and yet allowed me to begin. So, I'd also like to thank Jayson for being so gracious. I have nothing but respect for my opponent.

"The theme that Suzy Best, my running mate, and I have chosen is a simple one. Bobcat pride. It's simple, but it's also powerful. Go to the dictionary and you'll see 'pride' defined as 'a feeling, deep pleasure or satisfaction, derived from one's own achievements.' Note the word 'achievement.' Without pride, no achievement. Pride is that quality that, because we feel good about ourselves, allows us to achieve. In our middle school, that achievement can take many forms. I love athletics, so achieving excellence on the basketball court is especially important. I'm also a proud member—and captain—of our debate team. That's another area where pride motivates us to go that extra mile, do that extra research and work extra hard so that our team achieves, as it has, a national reputation.

"School pride is great, but so is family pride. I'm proud that my dad serves as mayor of this city and proud that my mom serves on the school board. I'm proud that Suzy's mom, Mrs. Laura Best, is president of the Bloom Historical Society. All my life I've been surrounded and inspired by achievers. These wonderful people serve as role models for all of us who strive to serve our school and community.

"I know this has been called a debate, but to be honest, I have no quarrels with Jayson. He's also an achiever. He has one of the highest grade point averages in school. He's a great addition to our basketball team. He always has a good word to say about everybody, and I'm sure today will be no different. Today is a day when our city can look at Bloom Middle School with pride. Bobcat pride. Bobcat pride is what makes us achievers. In my own way, I've tried to be an achiever. The same is true of Suzy, our head cheerleader, and a member of the honor society. Suzy and I will be honored to lead all of us to greater achievements. We hope that our achievements merit your vote. And we hope you will believe us when we say we want to achieve more—for our school, our families, and the community of Bloom."

Mack stops here. Immediate standing ovation. He smiles and nods in my direction. My turn. I walk to the mic and take a breath. There are two TV cameras, but I know, following Mack's example, to look into the one where the light is red.

"I w-w-w-w-w-want to first thank Mack for s-s-s-s-saying nice things about me. I also want to say that I didn't have t-t-t-to stutter on the word 'want' but I stuttered on purpose. That's because I w-w-w-wanted to get this stuttering issue out of the way. Not long ago, I would have hoped and prayed I could get through this s-s-s-s-s-s-speech without stuttering once. That was a dream of mine. But no more. I'm s-s-s-s-someone who stutters. And I'm okay with that. And even though our posters say 'We are not afraid,' right now I'm v-v-v-v-v-very afraid. I'm a-a-a-a-a-a-a-a-afraid of being on

TV. I'm afraid of not b-b-b-being able to get out a word. So, if that's true—and it is—why do our posters say 'We are not afraid'? Because we are not a-a-a-a-afraid of being afraid. We think it's okay to b-b-b-b-be afraid.

"Mack spoke about pride and achievements. All g-g-g-good things. But he spoke in broad generalities. I want to speak in specifics. I w-w-w-want to say what I b-b-b-believe has to change in our school and community—and why students like Gloria and myself are not afraid to call out those ch-ch-ch-changes. Gloria deserves m-m-m-most of the credit because she motivated our f-f-f-fellow students around our s-s-separate issues and what they have in c-c-common. And that is that w-w-we all n-n-need to be heard. That brings me to the first point of a four-point plan that Gloria and I w-w-w-want to initiate as your class officers.

"Point one: We will s-s-s-select a committee of students from all different backgrounds to help resolve disputes in student organizations. Gloria and I will lead the committee, and when we come up with a r-r-r-report, we will take it to the school b-b-b-board and ask that they c-c-c-c-c-c-c-consider our changes.

"Point two: We w-w-w-w-will recommend that the board consider ch-ch-ch-changing the Bloom Middle School budget funding. The m-m-m-money that goes to paying for out-of-s-s-s-state trips for our sports teams could instead be used to put in gender-neutral bathrooms. Everyone should be able to f-f-f-feel safe no matter how they identify. Most experts believe that gender is not binary. Our bathrooms should reflect that r-r-r-reality. If our sport teams want to play out of state, they c-c-c-can have their own f-f-f-f-fundraisers to pay for it. But I see gender-neutral bathrooms as a c-c-c-crucial part of our c-c-community—a w-w-w-way to make everyone f-f-feel comfortable and at home. And as president of the council, I'll p-p-p-petition the board to make that change.

"Point three: Let's m-m-m-make sure that students who want to debate—and, because of their personal speech, need more t-t-t-time to make their debate points—are g-g-g-g-given that time.

"Point four: The s-s-student c-c-c-council gets to challenge d-d-d-decisions made by the principal. We do that by g-g-g-g-getting to go before the school board and registering a s-s-s-s-s-strong complaint. We also think that wh-wh-wh-when we go before the school board those m-m-m-meetings should be made public. Anyone, including the press, can attend. That sh-sh-sh-should be true whether we're d-d-d-discussing our school funding or any other issue.

"I'll conclude by summarizing these f-f-f-four points into four words. We are not afraid. We are not afraid to h-h-h-have our voices heard. We are not afraid to push for ch-ch-ch-ch-changes important to us. We are not afraid to ch-ch-ch-challenge the old ways of doing things. We are not afraid of trying n-n-new things.

"Thank you for l-l-listening to me. Now that I have p-p-presented my plans, I know all of us w-w-w-want to hear the plans that Mack is p-p-p-proposing."

Before Mack can even stand back up, the auditorium breaks into cheers. It isn't just my friends and my dad. It's everyone. The cheers are loud and last for what feels like five minutes. I see the TV cameras whirl around to capture everyone on their feet, shouting as if I've scored the winning point at a basketball game. I feel great! I've said exactly what I wanted to say. What I needed to say. I don't care that I stuttered a lot. In fact, I've become comfortable with it. I may even like it. It's me, and it's honest.

Mack is at the microphone, about to respond. He's as confident as ever.

"Let me take my opponent's arguments point by point," he says. "Point one: Students running the school? Isn't that what the principal and the school board are for? What will happen if every freshman's busted locker door turns into a committee meeting? Shouldn't we spend our time learning and striving to be the best we can be, rather than making problems for those who are trying to do a job?

"After thinking about it, I don't have strong disagreements with Jayson's other three points. The world is changing. The world is becoming more accepting. And I can see the reasoning behind having neutral-gender bathrooms. And yes, we can look at our debate rules. And I absolutely think it's a smart move to let the school council go to the school board if the council has issues with the principal. And if you elect me president, that's just what I'll do.

"Jayson's platform is interesting, but his main point—of changing the way that disputes are settled in the school—isn't practical. It's not realistic. Students shouldn't be in charge. I say, let's concentrate on our studies, let's stick to winning championships, whether in basketball or debate, and let's be the best Bobcats we can be!"

Another round of applause.

But I'm ready to fire back.

"Well," I say, "it's g-g-g-g-great that Mack and I agree on so many things. I'm g-g-g-g-glad he's adopted most of my plans. I say that b-b-b-because Mack is such a smart guy and a good person to have on your team. And because he's smart, he has to understand that I'm not s-s-s-saying that students should be able to bring the whole school to a halt with every little complaint. All I'm s-s-s-saying is that students have the r-r-r-right to question decisions. We should have the r-r-r-right to bring those questions to the board. Of course, we won't make the final decision. The board will. But our voice will be h-h-h-h-heard.

"Mack summed up, and I'd like to sum up as well. I'm not against Bobcat pride. I'm on the basketball t-t-t-team, and I f-f-f-feel that pride when I play. I also f-f-f-feel pride when Mack makes the w-w-w-winning shots. Pride is a beautiful thing. But there's a b-b-b-big difference between pride and change. Mack is c-c-c-calling for more pride, and I s-s-say yes. But he's n-n-n-not giving you a plan for change. That's where we d-d-d-disagree. I'm for change. I'm not afraid of change. I know many of you want change and know we need change. And if y-y-you're not afraid of change, I say, 'Vote Linden and Lopez! We are not afraid!'"

I get another standing ovation. It's hard to tell whether it's louder or longer than Mack's ovation. But it's strong. Dad is hugging Gloria's parents. Gloria has tears in her eyes. Chuck is jumping up and down, along with his mom and Big Al. Dr. Dan is shaking hands with Sylvia. The rest of my squad are screaming and clapping.

No matter what happens next, I'm proud of myself.

CHAPTER 36

And Your President Is . . .

The day before Thanksgiving is always exciting. The holiday season has officially arrived, we have the next day off, we have big meals with families to look forward to. Election Day only adds to the excitement.

By the time I arrive, there is already a line from the gym door and down the hallway. Monitors stand by two big boxes in the hallway to make sure each student drops a single ballot through the slot.

Voting ends promptly at 10:00 a.m. to allow enough time for the tally. At the end of the day, we'll be called to the auditorium and read the results.

Each class period crawls by. I look at the clock as much as I look at the teacher. In third-period geometry, Mr. Gully calls my name three times before I respond. Luckily, I'm not alone. No one else can concentrate on class either. Even the teachers are having trouble focusing on their lessons. Once the voting ends at 10:00 a.m., everyone starts predicting. Everyone is whispering. Mack's gonna win in a landslide. Gloria will upset Suzy. I'm gonna win big. I'm gonna lose big. The debate made Mack look great. The debate helped me more. The debate hurt me. The issues I brought up really matter. The issues don't matter. The chatter never stops. I have no idea what's going to happen. One minute I'm hopeful. The next minute I'm not. I have no idea. All I know is that I'm really nervous. At lunchtime, my friends and I can't talk about anything else.

Then, finally, at the start of our last class, Principal Goodman's voice comes over the loudspeaker.

"Listen up, Bobcats. Due to scheduling conflicts, I'm canceling our usual all-school meeting in the auditorium and will simply announce the results now."

Suddenly I get scared. My heart starts racing. Why the change? Could it be that Principal Goodman, along with Mack's parents—the mayor and mayor's wife, who serves on the school board—have messed with the votes? Are they capable of that? My hope is starting to fade. I remember that Mack's the most popular kid at school. Even if I did win the debate, as some have said, you can win a debate and lose an election. Why would Principal Goodman want to make the announcement over the PA system and not in person?

Even Gloria warned me. After the debate, after I'd gone home, she called to say that, yes, I did well. And yes, she felt like I had gotten my points across. And yes, kids had reacted positively.

"I just don't w-w-want you to be disappointed," she said. "I think we have a chance—a decent chance—but we don't really know, do w-w-we?"

"You think Mack and Suzy c-c-c-could win in a land-slide?"

"Anything is p-p-possible."

Gloria's words are coming back to me—*anything is possible*—as I wait for Principal Goodman to read the results.

I hold my breath and think, *Whatever happens, I am not afraid.*

He says, "For vice president, Suzy Best received 120 votes and Gloria Lopez 450 votes."

A huge cheer erupts.

"But the race for president," states the principal, "was much closer."

Now I can't breathe.

"Mack Gaines got 283 votes, and Jayson Linden . . . 287. Congratulations to Gloria and Jayson, our new class president and vice president. That is all. Happy Thanksgiving."

WHOOOOOOOOOA!

I can hardly believe it. I race out of the classroom, and so does everyone else. The hallways are packed. Someone starts shouting, "Linden and Lopez! We are not afraid!" And everyone joins in. "We are not afraid! We are not afraid!" In the middle of it all, I find Chuck, Preeda, Gino, and Amia. Everyone's jumping up and down.

"Close," says Chuck, "but man, it doesn't make any difference. You did it!"

Gloria comes running up to me and gives me a big hug.

"You're the big winner," I tell her. "You won by a l-l-l-landslide!"

"A win is a win," she says. "Enjoy it! We did it together! The real work begins after Th-Th-Thanksgiving."

"We are not afraid!" everyone kept chanting. "We are not afraid!"

Out of the crowd, Mack shows up and walks over to me.

"Great job, Jayson. You won fair and square." He holds out his hand for me to shake.

I take it and pump it up and down. "Thanks, Mack. I'm

g-g-g-gonna need your help to make some of these changes."

"I have a lot of respect for you, Jayson. I know you'll do a great job."

Behind him, I see Suzy congratulating Gloria.

It's the best day of school. Ever. And I can't wait for all the ways we're going to change our school for the better—together.

ACKNOWLEDGMENTS

I am so grateful to have had the opportunity to write this book with David Ritz. In the beginning, meeting President Biden and others, it all seemed like a dream. I have had a lot going on these past few years and I am so glad to have had the opportunity to further support people who stutter and write a story about kids who stutter, yet lead normal lives.

I would first like to acknowledge my agent, David Vigliano. He believed in this book before any of us did. He is the main reason this book was made. If it had not been for him taking the initiative to contact my parents out of the blue, it never would have happened.

Thank you to Megan Ilnitzki from HarperCollins. Megan was at my side throughout the process. Thank you for all the support and suggestions!

My speech therapist, Laura Darling, was a big part of my growth as a person and of this book. She began working with me when I was in third grade and throughout middle school. She is the best! She showed me a whole different way to look at stuttering. She helped me grow from a scared boy into a happy teenager who embraces his stutter!

I would also like to thank all my friends for always being

there for me when I had my rough times and my good times. They never treated me as someone who was different. I am so grateful for all of them.

Thank you to all the stuttering groups who reached out when this all began. They taught me that I was never alone. I would like to thank the Stuttering Association for the Young (SAY), FRIENDS: The National Association for Young People Who Stutter, and Schneider Speech all for taking the time to reach out and believe in me and all others who stutter.

I would also like to acknowledge President Biden. He was a huge part of my journey with stuttering. He was so kind and showed so much empathy toward me. He also showed me that stuttering does not define me and never will!

It was so great to work with David Ritz. Not only was he a great creative partner, he is also a person who stutters. He gets it! Thank you, David, for being such a big part of bringing a true voice and story to Jayson, Gloria, and the stuttering community as a whole.

Finally, I want to thank my family. Without you, none of this would have happened. Without you all, I wouldn't be able to share with everyone that our imperfections are truly our gifts.

—Brayden Harrington